It wasn't that she disliked him

How could she dislike someone whom she knew marginally less than the postman. No. He seemed reasonable enough, if a shade daunting. It was the fact that she felt beholden to him, tied to him by compulsory gratitude, that was so irksome.

"You're looking pretty savage," Darcy said, "as though you were planning something highly unpleasant and not altogether legal. But I'll give you the benefit of the doubt."

He flustered her. "Look," she said, "I'm grateful for everything you've done, and if I can make it up to you I—"

"Oh, you can," he muttered meaningfully, his intensely blue eyes fixed firmly on her, "and you will."

Sally St. John lives with her husband and daughter in "the back of beyond in Wales," steeped in animals—dog, cats, rabbit, guinea pig and guinea fowl. She is a member of Radnorshire Wildlife Trust, Friends of the Earth and The Woodland Trust. Before marriage her career went through various short-order jobs: shop assistant, laboratory assistant, chamber maid, occupational therapist. Later she was student assistant stage manager at Harrogate Opera House and eventually became an actress. She played the part of Julia Kirby in the very first program Yorkshire Television produced, *Tom Grattan's War*, which was filmed on location in Yorkshire. She played other TV roles through the years, but retired to bring up her daughter. She enjoys travel (but not flying), classical music, living in the country and interesting cooking.

STUDY
IN LOVE

Sally St. John

Harlequin Books

TORONTO • NEW YORK • LONDON
AMSTERDAM • PARIS • SYDNEY • HAMBURG
STOCKHOLM • ATHENS • TOKYO • MILAN

Original hardcover edition published in 1989
by Mills & Boon Limited

ISBN 0-373-17068-8

Harlequin Romance first edition August 1990

CHAPTER ONE

'HELLO again, my darling.'

The warm breath from his whisper sent a tremor down Jem's neck as she turned apprehensively. He was too close. Her attempted smile faltered and died miserably. What could she say to this man, in name so intimate, in fact as alien to her as the Man from Mars?

'Good morning, Mr Lister,' she answered loudly, praying that no one in the crowded art school vestibule had overheard his greeting. 'Nice to meet you again.'

The sudden rush of blood to her cheeks belied Jem's casual words and she saw, with alarm, the gleam of sardonic humour behind Darcy Lister's brilliant blue eyes. He must know her confidence was a sham.

'Six months is a long time,' he murmured. 'How have I managed to live without you?'

'Please, Mr Lister,' she hissed, moving hurriedly away from a clutch of new students diffidently eyeing the notice-board. 'Please keep your voice down, you know we said——'

'I do think, under the circumstances, you could call me Darcy, don't you?' He blandly ignored her, seeming to revel in the discomfiture he was causing.

'I wish we'd never done it now!' she groaned as one or two pairs of curious eyes followed her across the lofty Edwardian hall of the London School of Art. She tried to escape him by pretending to search through a heap of class registers by the main entrance.

'No regrets, Jemima. We have. There's no going back now.'

'I know, I know,' she muttered through her teeth, 'but there's no need to broadcast it like the town crier. As you said at the time, it's purely business, and we'd both look pretty daft if it got out.'

'Would we?' he asked, staring down at her piercingly. 'I think maybe *I* would, but I'm not so sure about you. . .' He let the grey cloud of ambiguity hang between them.

Six months ago, when the plan had been executed, this first day of her postgraduate sculpture course had seemed a million miles away. The consequence had been something to view down a telescope, distant, unthreatening. Now it had arrived and she realised that no amount of forethought could have prepared her for the ordeal of the reality.

It wasn't that she disliked him. How could she dislike someone whom she knew marginally less intimately than she knew the dustman? No. He seemed reasonable enough, if a shade daunting with that hair and those intensely blue eyes. It was the fact that she felt beholden to him, tied to him by compulsory gratitude, that was so irksome. It never entered her head how he might feel.

'You're looking pretty savage. Have they refused your grant after all our clandestine efforts?'

Jem drew her mind, like a reluctant cork, back to the moment. 'No, no, they paid me. . .thanks. I was just a wee bit preoccupied.'

'You looked as though you were planning something highly unpleasant and not altogether legal, but I'll give you the benefit of the doubt!'

He flustered her. She felt diminished by the sardonic

glint that lurked in his eyes. 'Look, I'm very grateful to you for everything you've done, and if I can make it up to you I——'

'Oh, you can,' he muttered meaningfully, neatly side-stepping a short young man clutching a cumbersome work of dubious art to his bosom, 'and you will.' The one black eyebrow he raised spoke volumes.

She felt a surge of misgiving. 'You sound very certain. What have you in mind?'

But he just grinned, stretching out his hand to ruffle her cropped head dismissively. 'Later, darling, later,' he murmured provocatively, and turned abruptly, parting the sea of students before him like a latter-day Moses and disappeared into the throng, leaving Jem more than a little baffled.

He seemed to come and go through her life like the Demon King, she thought: a puff of green smoke and he was gone. Or come!

As Jem pressed her way through the claustrophobic swell of bright, bizarre students, the image of Darcy Lister's first pantomime entrance into her life returned to her.

That had been six months ago, on a washout of a day in late April. When a penetrating drizzle had stuck her spiky hair to her head as if she were in a swimwear ad and she had had to cycle the marathon journey from Stoke Newington to the centre of London for an interview. April the twenty-third. Make or break day.

Facing the Bursaries Committee of the London School of Art to see if she was eligible for a grant to continue her studies in the next academic year had been worse than any prisoner brought before the parole board ever had to endure.

Her history, her future, hopes, aspirations, bank

balance and the great-grandparents of her cat were all
delved into remorselessly and, after much sage nodding, found lacking.

'I am *very* sorry, Miss Selby. It seems that you don't
quite come within the scope of *any* of our bursaries. It
looks as if we shall, reluctantly, have to turn you down.
It is a great shame because you are indeed a very
promising sculptress. . .but perhaps in another couple
of years you will have settled down and got married,
and then you could apply for the Julia Maudsby
Award.'

'I don't understand,' Jem croaked miserably, fighting
back the tears of injustice.

The chairman elaborated, smiling helpfully into her
enormous eyes. 'The Maudsby Postgraduate Award for
married women. To encourage you ladies to leave the
home and the babies and take up full-time education
again. Julia Maudsby stipulated that no regard what-
soever was to be taken of the husband's earnings, to
afford the recipient complete independence from any
opposition he might express. Most laudable. A far-
sighted lady, Mrs Maudsby. Way ahead of her time.'

His patronising unction drew a shudder from Jem.
Holding her head as high as five-foot two would allow,
she groped blindly towards the door, accumulated tears
overflowing as she leaned flaccidly against the wall of
the corridor, her world a crumbling ruin.

'You must be April, weeping her girlish tears. Am I
right?' The bantering words came out of the blue.
Lifting streaming eyes, she had blinked, trying to focus
on the voice's source. It was a long way up, and
blurred. A large hanky was thrust insistently into her
hand and she at last glimpsed him. He was tall, slim,

his eyes and hair startling enough to surprise her out of her wallowing self-pity.

The hair was burnished silver, mellow in the dim corridor, and the eyes a deep, intense blue beneath strongly arched black brows. Yet the face was young, no more than early thirties, Jem fleetingly registered before her gaze fell to his stern, uncompromising mouth which had just the hint of a quirky smile disapearing from one corner. There was something distantly, disturbingly familiar about him but, try as she might, she couldn't place him.

'No, you're not April. You're Jemima Selby.' It was an accusation.

Jem nodded, surprised.

'I think you need a drink. Grab your things.' And he turned on his heel and strode along the corridor, confident that she would follow.

She did, thoroughly intrigued by this odd creature who had materialised at her side out of nowhere.

The pub round the corner from the college was unfamiliar to Jem. It was a regular lunchtime haunt for the boozier faction of her year but, apart from not having the money to waste on endless rounds of drinks, Jem had always found herself too wrapped up in her work to break off and socialise.

She was known as a loner, dedicated and undoubtedly talented, but a little dotty. Putting Art, with a capital A, before Real Life. And indeed she did find it easier to talk about art and things related to it. Sticking to a treatise on the relative merits of Patrick Procktor and David Hockney was safer than trying to plunge head-first into the ferment of sex and freaky clothes, which seemed to be all that was ever discussed.

All of which explained why she had begun to feel

pretty nervous sitting in the nearly empty bar, swept clean of near-miss Madonnas and U2 look-alikes by the advent of the Easter holidays, waiting for the silver-haired man to reappear. What was she going to *say* to him? The weather would obviously not keep him spellbound, so what were they going to talk about?

She wasn't left to languish in suspense for long!

'Perhaps,' he had begun, placing a double brandy before her, 'the best thing would be if I were to marry you.'

CHAPTER TWO

AFTER the initial shock Jem had recovered quickly. She might have known, she'd thought furiously, lunging for the fisherman's tackle basket that served her as a handbag. A weirdo. Fancy allowing herself to be conned like that! But he hadn't seemed the type. Then again, how would she know? She'd probably have entertained Dr Crippen and been none the wiser.

She was doubly angry with herself on finding that she'd trapped herself in a corner behind the table, and was desperately crabbing her way along the seat trying to escape when he sat down, blocking her exit.

'Excuse me!' She found it difficult to sound snooty while quaking with fright. 'I wish to leave.'

He raised his eyes to heaven. 'Come on, what are you? A canny art student or a shrinking violet? I'm not trying anything on, and even if I were, we're pretty public for that kind of thing.'

Not precisely reassured, but at least acknowledging the truth of what he said, she eased her way back into her corner, trying to devise an alternative getaway.

'No. Heaven knows why I'm doing this. Is it "Be kind to strays" week?' He paused and, when she made no move to reply, added, 'You're going to have to leave college if you don't get some money, aren't you?'

Despite herself, Jem nodded. Perhaps, after all, he wasn't just some kook wandering in off the streets. Perhaps he really did have something to do with the college. How else would he know her name?

'Well, Jemima——'

'Jem,' she corrected automatically, ready to bite off her tongue immediately at her own foolishness.

'Well, Jem?' He gave her a long, cool look as her eyes blazed at him belligerently out of a pinched, undernourished face.

'I know I'm not a prepossessing sight, but there's no need to stare at me like that!' she burst out, running a small, cracked hand through hair that looked as if it had been styled by an inept hedger and ditcher with a blunt billhook.

'I'm not,' he said wearily. 'I just think you should tell me all about it, and we'll see what we can do to assist you.'

'I'm not telling you anything,' she muttered bluntly. 'I don't even know who you are.'

'My name is Darcy Lister. I'm a painter.'

She gasped, her dim recognition instantly clarified by his name. Of course that was who he was. Darcy Lister. The most famous British artist of the decade. She'd seen his photo countless times, but in the flesh he'd deceived her with his sheer size and vitality. His photographs didn't do him justice.

'Oh, and of course, you're Principal Guest Lecturer in Painting and Life Drawing at the college this coming year. I understand now!' That was why he'd been prowling the corridor. He'd had every right to be. She felt her attitude towards him change subtly. Suspicion changed to disbelief that someone so lofty should condescend to take an interest in her.

'But—but why. . .? I mean, you'd be prepared to. . .marry me?' The last words came out as a pathetic squeak. 'Why?'

'For you to qualify for the Maudsby Award. But no

more questions. Before I commit myself I want to find out everything that there is to know about you.'

It was a command and Jem held her tongue, but she couldn't stop her thoughts from running riot. Where had he materialised from? Why had he suddenly latched on to her? How did he know all these things about her?

The idea that he might marry her was so fantastic, she tried to dismiss it from her mind, but the tantalising picture of her future if she were awarded the Julia Maudsby Scholarship kept insinuating itself into view. Two whole years with enough money to indulge all her artistic whims. It was extremely tempting. . .

Yet it baffled her that he should think her worth considering. She was hardly eye-catching, she conceded, and it was obvious to even the blindest optimist that she hadn't swept him off his feet with her beauty, charm and wit. She eyed him obliquely, pondering on what possible reason he could have for this sudden outlandish scheme.

Confused and excited, she took an unaccustomed gulp of brandy. Cardiac arrest nearly resulted as it detonated, in series, all the way down to her stomach. Exasperatedly, Darcy Lister slapped her back as she fought for breath and gripped the table-edge like a drowning sailor on a life-raft. Heavens, what an exhibition she was making of herself! She just wasn't used to excitement on this scale. Being singled out for attention was something she shrank from, and to find herself suddenly of such interest to the world—first the committee, then Darcy Lister, and now the curious in the taproom of a public house, all in one day—was too much.

She subsided against the backrest, resigned to the

third degree, willing it to be over as soon as possible so that she could escape again into being a nonentity.

'Why have you no money?' the first question was barked at her.

'Because I've spent it all.'

'Yes, yes. . .but where did it originate, and why is there no more forthcoming?'

It really went against the grain to discuss her private affairs like this, but she supposed that if a famous artist like Darcy Lister was showing such flattering interest in her, the least she could do was respond. 'My grandmother gave it to me, and now she's got none left.'

'That's your grandmother in the Virgin Islands? The Caribbean grandmother?'

He knew that, too? 'I've only got one. . .but, how did you——?'

'Never mind that now,' he interrupted tersely. 'Why didn't you apply to your government for a grant if there's no more money available from the family? Surely they would be able to help you?'

She laughed mirthlessly. 'If you've heard about my "Caribbean Grandmother" you *must* have come across my "Unusual Circumstances" too.'

'No. What are they?'

The bitterness of past struggles rose up again and marred the melodious depth of Jem's voice. 'They won't give me a grant because, by a quirk of fate, I was born on the wrong island and I'm not entitled to one.'

Darcy groaned and ran a lean hand impatiently through his hair. 'This is worse than trying to milk a bull! Why don't you just start at the beginning and go through it all till you get to the end? And don't be so damned coy. I'm not from the Inland Revenue!'

A brief smile illuminated her face, leaving an iridescent impression of impishness slowly fading across the wan features. 'All right,' she sighed, 'but it's a long story.'

She took a more tentative sip at her brandy and began, hesitantly at first, then slowly gaining confidence as the odd story unfolded.

'When I was born my father had already been dead for six months. Grandma says he was a waster. . .but then, she was prejudiced. He drank too much and liked the women. Also, apparently he'd gambled away half the sugar estate that my mother owned jointly with my grandmother. As you can imagine, Grandma didn't like him, and when it turned out he'd shot himself one night when he was drunk she said she couldn't find it in her heart to be sorry. Does that shock you? It did me at first, when I was little, but I've heard so many things since that I think perhaps it was for the best.

'Certainly the doctors said that my mother died of a broken heart after I was born because of all the unhappiness he'd caused her. She was from Tortola, like him. That's the main island of the *British* Virgin Islands, you know. Some people don't know that there are two kinds, British and American.

'Well, that's where my "Unusual Circumstances" arose! My mother had to be rushed to St Croix, one of the American islands, because my birth was causing complications that they couldn't cope with on Tortola, so I was born, to all intents and purposes, in America.

'When my mother died two days later the hospital authorities registered me as an American citizen and Grandma, not thinking it would make much difference, didn't bother to make me British as well.'

She heaved a great sigh, loath to blame her grandmother, whose self-sacrifice had amply repaid the seemingly small omission, but sorry that a little foresight could have saved so much trouble.

'I was brought up on Tortola by my grandmother. She struggled to keep what was left of the estate going, but sugar went through a rough time round about then and we were very poor. And when, eventually, I was accepted into college here she had to sell the last bit of valuable land and all her jewellery to pay my way.

'You see, because I was officially a foreigner, the grant people in Tortola couldn't offer me money, and because I was living "abroad" according to the American authorities, and didn't comply with the legal residency requirements for American citizens, neither could they. I was well and truly in a cleft stick. . .and still am.'

The gloom of her situation descended on her once more, and the optimistic spark engendered by Darcy Lister's outrageous offer fizzled out with a dull phut.

How silly she was to believe him. He was having a bit of sport at her expense and very soon he'd get bored and go away. And leave her, after that brief fool's paradise, marginally more depressed than she had been before.

However, he hadn't shown immediate signs of abandoning her. 'Well, what about the British Government here, or the London education people? Surely you come under their jurisdiction?'

'No. I've tried them, but they "deeply regret" that, as I am a foreign student, and as they have so *many* other calls on their cash, *and* due to education cuts, et cetera, et cetera—you name it, they said it—they can't help me either.

'In fact, I stirred up quite a hornet's nest, because they started making discreet enquiries as to whether or not I could support myself and if I was doing any illegal work. *All* work is illegal if you're a foreign student,' she added to forestall his obvious question, 'so I've drawn attention to myself that I could well have done without. Now I wouldn't even be able to get a job waitressing to pay my way or they'd have me deported.'

'Surely,' he remarked, with comfortable ignorance, 'it wouldn't be so bad to have to go back to Tortola? It's an idyllic spot, from what I've heard.'

'Idyllic if you don't have to earn a living,' she muttered bitterly. 'Oh, I could always become a chambermaid, I suppose, doubling up as a limbo dancer in the evenings.' A rueful laugh escaped her. 'No doubt I'd earn more money than puddling away at plaster of Paris but, hell, the boredom. You've no idea. It's a cultural desert.' She shrugged fatalistically. 'It would be fine if I had established myself with a decent reputation here in Britain and could work and sell my sculptures from Tortola, but I'm unknown, and nobody's going to risk travelling the three thousand odd miles to get there only to find it's "not quite what they're looking for, thank you". . .are they?'

'What a heart-rending picture that conjures up!' he sneered brutally. 'The downtrodden artist starving in a garret has taken on a new dimension. But it seems to me,' he added, eyeing her disparagingly, 'as if aspiration has given way to self-pity. You sound defeated before the battle's even been joined.'

Jem was livid. 'I am not defeated!' she spluttered, ignoring his patronising expression. 'I just don't have the money to come back to college next year and do two years postgraduate. . .can't you understand?' She paused, trying to calm herself. 'I'm having to eke out what I've got left—which isn't very much—like some demented Scrooge as it is, but I *can't* make it last two more years. It'll stretch to September, and then that's it. *Finis!*' She sighed exaggeratedly. 'I'm sorry if I'm disappointingly Chekhovian. It's very difficult to seem animated when the rent's in arrears and your life's ambition has just done a pratfall into oblivion!'

'A very apt expression, Miss Selby,' he muttered brusquely. 'And what do you propose to do about it?'

She stared at him blankly, heaved another great sigh and whispered dolefully, 'I don't know.'

There was a pause as he obviously fought a brief struggle with exasperation and staged a remarkable victory. 'OK. Let's change tack, shall we? What do you hope to gain by adding two years to your studies? And, more importantly, what about afterwards? What about the future?'

Jem squirmed under the cross-examination. But at least she could answer him with some degree of confidence this time. She knew exactly what her future would be.

'I'm going to earn my living as a sculptor,' she said decisively. 'It's my life. I know I'm good,' she added without the slightest conceit, 'though I do lack commercial polish, I know. My stuff's raw round the edges just yet, but, you see, that's why I have to do the postgrad. I've *got* to perfect my techniques, work at smoothing out all the faults, and at the same time develop the emotions that I feel grow deeper and stronger with every piece I do.'

Suddenly she felt lost in her dream. Darcy and the pub had dematerialised. 'And when I've made a name for myself and I'm completely independent, *then* I shall go back to Tortola and release my grandmother from the subservience she's been forced into on my account, so that she never has to work again. I will never, *never* live the kind of dead-end existence my parents suffered and which killed them both. I shall flower on a different stalk and bear the kind of fruit that will endure and still be seen and talked about when I'm long dead. You see, I want to be an artist. Living, breathing and working art, and I don't care how long it takes me. I shall do it.

'That's how I see my future, Mr Lister.'

She had surprised herself with her own openness. After all, they were strictly secret ambitions, and she'd told no one else of her deep convictions in her own talent.

But strangely, watching Darcy Lister's reaction, she felt none of the embarrassed squirmings she'd expected from speaking her mind. He sat, utterly relaxed, eyeing her keenly from the shadows where the seductive—or so the landlord hoped—red lighting failed to penetrate, looking as if it were the most natural thing to listen to impassioned self-publicity.

'And with no money,' his low voice reached her from the gloom, 'you'll have to return home to obscurity and hopelessness in that haven of tourism for the rich and philistine. Is that correct?'

Something in the cadence of his voice gave her pause as she nodded. A conspiratorial undertone. Could he possibly be serious about this loony scheme? He hadn't mentioned it again, but it was too intriguing to just dismiss. There was only one way to find out.

'Can I ask you a few questions now? I think I deserve a return bout!'

He gave a flippant gesture, as if to say 'What have I

got to lose?' and, producing a tiny pad and pencil from the back pocket of his jeans, he appeared to withdraw into himself and began sketching the plasterwork moulding round the ceiling.

Thanks a lot! Jem thought bitterly, but her voice held no ire as she asked, 'How do you know so much about me?'

'College records,' he mumbled round the pencil between his teeth as he vigorously wielded a rubber. 'I'm supposed to be enlightening the callow in anatomy and life drawing at your precious college next academic year. I have to make some kind of effort at getting to know a few of the more promising ones. Next?'

Damn him! she thought, getting flustered. He's making this as difficult as he can. 'Next' indeed!

'Well, how do you know about the Bursaries Committee turning me down? You weren't in the room, and they didn't rush out with a proclamation to nail to the gate. So, who told you?'

He looked up speculatively at that. 'I was in the secretary's office asking the pneumatic Miss Jessop for a date, and the connecting door happened to be open. . .quite simple really!'

Jem had secretly hoped for something a bit more flattering than that, but the prosaic reality was no more than could be expected.

'Well, why the interest?' she asked, somewhat bluntly. 'I'm not the first, and I'm certain I won't be the last, to be found wanting by those with their hands on the purse-strings.'

'Ah, but I won't be eavesdropping on them, will I?'

True! she thought. So where do we go from here? I can't just baldly ask him if he meant what he said. . .I'm not even sure now that he did say it!

'And,' he added smoothly, 'they won't be nearly as talented or intriguing, I should imagine, and I won't be in the same reckless mood. So make the most of it. I meant what I said. . .though heaven knows why. I'm offering you a marriage of convenience to enable you to get that bursary. Yes or no?'

'I don't know you.' Jem was playing for time.

'No, and you probably never will. This is purely business, first and last.'

'But what happens when I've got the money? How do we go about ending the arrangement?' She wasn't able to bring herself to mention it as marriage. The whole episode was beginning to strike her with its enormity.

'Leave all that to me,' Darcy said calmly. 'You can rest assured I shan't want to prolong the situation any more than necessary. And if I've read your character correctly, you yourself will provide the perfect get-out. But if not. . .well. . .we'll just have to wait out the year and divorce. We can either separate for two years and then apply or you can divorce me straight away on grounds of unreasonable behaviour. I won't contest it. No harm in that, is there?'

'But I don't want a divorce,' Jem whispered plaintively, 'When, or should I say *if*, I marry I want it to be for real. I want to love the man I marry and I. . .' suddenly she found it difficult to meet his gaze '. . .I. . .want him to. . .love me.' She carried on in a headlong rush. 'I know you're doing this out of the goodness of your heart, but——'

'I'm sorry to disillusion you,' he interrupted harshly, 'but you're wrong. I haven't got a heart, so don't try heaping sentimental motives on me. I'm offering you this because I dislike seeing exceptional talent thrown down the drain for a technicality.'

He leaned over the table towards her, silver hair flashing in the ruby light. 'Marriage is a sacred cow, love. An anachronism. How on earth, in this upside-down world, can a girl possibly decide one day that the simpering twerp beside her at the altar is the man she wants to spend her life with? For all she knows he'll be influenced by some highbrow programme on Channel Four a couple of weeks later and decide that, really, he'd be better off as a transvestite. You just don't know. There's no permanence, no guarantee.'

'I think that's a very sad attitude to have,' she remarked unhappily. 'No wonder you can take this offer of yours so lightly.'

'I'm not taking it lightly. I'm in real earnest. The sort of marriage we'd have could only be classed, at best, as a paper transaction. There'd be no danger of there being any expectations on either side that couldn't be met. I wouldn't be demanding my conjugal rights, my socks washed and three square meals a day.'

'Just as well. I can't cook!' Jem confessed, secretly far more relieved about the sexual side of their pro-posed liaison. At least with that looming obstruction out of the way the idea didn't seem so daunting.

There certainly wouldn't be any comfortable senti-ment associated with the tie but, after all, what did she really want from life? Security and stagnation, or the freedom and fulfilment of a life and career that would be wholly her own. . .apart from the initial boost from Darcy Lister's name.

What the hell? That was all it was, wasn't it? The temporary use of a name. She was a child of the eighties. Why not be bold? Gamble her single status on the bursary stakes.

After all, she told herself, what risk could there be? I don't own anything, so I won't lose anything when we divorce. There'll be no complications. No property or children to wrangle over. There'll be nothing but advantage. . .for me at least——A sudden thought struck her.

'What will you get out of all this, though? Everything seems to be stacked in my favour. What about you?'

'Oh, I'll think of something, don't worry. . .But you can rest assured,' he promised swiftly as he saw alarm flash across her face, 'that it'll be perfectly harmless. To do with work only, and that's something you'll sympathise with, I'm sure.

'So. . .are you going to be steely and decisive and get married for Julia Maudsby, or are you going to remain a Miss Wet Nellie all your life? Which is it to be?'

Leaving herself no time to think better of it, like a Christmas bather in the Serpentine, she blurted, 'I want you to marry me. . .please,' and was immediately beset by all the objections she had been too *distraite* to comtemplate before.

'Sensible girl,' said Darcy, ignoring the fact that she had a hand pressed over her mouth as if to ward off a bout of vomiting. 'Now then, how soon, and where?'

The details of how to reach Hammersmith Register Office, how they could contact one another and sundry others all seemed to be accomplished at breathtaking speed, and Jem had found herself out on the street alone, with the final sound of the landlord bolting the pub door firmly on her past forever. She was committed now, whether she liked it or not.

The wedding itself, five days later, had been an unsentimental affair. It had been bedevilled by form filling, Jem's foreignness adding to the red tape of a special licence. It was then that Darcy had suggested she apply for British nationality while she had the opportunity. Being married to him would facilitate that added bonus!

She had felt no emotion as he had placed a ring on her finger—that he should retrieve it afterwards had been previously agreed upon. So this is marriage, went through her head as she signed her name for the umpteenth time. Jemima Jane Selby marries Darcy Giles Lister on this twenty-eighth day of April. Well. . .how odd!

Darcy had waved an airy farewell on the Register Office steps and Jem had caught the tube to her 'single unit dwelling', otherwise known as a bedsit, to begin her new life as Mrs Lister. . .Alone.

CHAPTER THREE

SITTING now beside the tall, gaunt window of the life class, the brontosaurian radiator clicking loudly in the lofty silence, Jem shifted slightly on the hard wooden donkey she was working at. Restlessly, she cast her eyes around the old room.

Everyone seemed to be getting on so well with Darcy Lister and yet, whenever he came close to her, Jem found herself tensing. Hoping against hope that he would turn away before he reached her. I never imagined that being married to him was going to make life so difficult! she fumed to herself, avoiding his eye for the hundredth time that afternoon.

A hefty sigh disturbed the cathedral calm, drawing her back to reality. The model was getting restive.

Concert hall coughing broke out as the Anne of Cleves clone descended from her dais and modestly draped herself in a vast Japanese kimono. It was hot in the room, to save her the discomfort of terminal goose-pimples, and the new lecturer, cool in shirt sleeves, began once again circulating among the scattered easels, eyeing work, saying nothing.

Jem removed her gold-rimmed glasses, trying to appear inconspicuous as the prowling figure moved inexorably closer.

'We meet again, wife!'

'You'd better stop this!' Jem whispered fiercely as the tall elegance of the 'Lecturer in Life' loomed over her. 'That was part of the arrangement, remember? That we don't let on to anyone.'

'I just like playing the cat occasionally. You make such a rewarding mouse.' The lowering light from outside caught the gleam of mockery in his eye. 'Let's take a look at Ida here. How are you getting on with her?' and he bent over her drawing.

'Oh. . .well. . .I'm struggling.'

'I can tell!' Darcy muttered sarcastically, sitting on Jem's donkey facing the easel. 'She looks as if she's made out of steel plate. What have you done to her?'

Jem peered miserably over his shoulder, fumbling for her glasses so that she could see what he was talking about. She hadn't thought that her life drawing was quite that bad. A little stiff maybe, and leaning on an inclined plane rather than draped elegantly over a chaise-longue, but certainly not back to first-year standard.

'I haven't quite got back into practice,' she said feebly, hooking herself up to sight again. 'The summer break is too long.'

'Rubbish, my dear Jemima, and double rubbish.' A harsh disapproval overlaid his voice. 'What the hell do you think you're given long vacations for? The good of your health?

'No!' he mowed through her open-mouthed amazement. 'They're for work. . .consolidation. Seeing this infantile effort fills me with the deepest suspicion. The stuff you showed me six months ago was streets ahead of this. Are you sure that that was *your* work?'

A knot in her stomach rapidly grew from a pebble of incredulity into a boulder of indigestible anger. 'Are you trying to imply that I cheated?' she spluttered. 'Because——'

'Oh,' he brushed her pink-cheeked explosion aside

airily, 'I've known it happen often. Students are always trying to pass off other people's work as their own. There's no way of checking.' He paused, seeing the stricken look that crossed her face, and softened his tone slightly. 'I'm not saying *you* have, but certainly the contrast between this and your other stuff is too great for there not to be some damned good reason. Come! Out with it!'

The brusqueness of his manner tautened her sagging nerve. 'Well, I doubt whether even you would be overly creative on a diet of porridge for three weeks. That's what you have to live on when you've got no money!'

'No money? What happened to Julia Maudsby? You can't have spent it all, surely?'

'The Julia Maudsby Scholarship,' Jem intoned icily, retreating behind her glasses, 'or any other scholarship, as you well know, is paid on the first day of term—today. And as my grandmother's money finally ran out three weeks ago I've been fairly hand to mouth ever since. I think I managed pretty well up till then, though.' She allowed herself a small smile of self-congratulation. 'I didn't owe anybody anything.'

'You could have gone to Social Security. They'd have tided you over till today, surely? I can't understand——'

'I'm married to you!'

'I don't see the connection.'

'Civil Service conventions dictate that husbands support their wives. They don't encompass marriages of convenience, or anything the slightest bit unconventional. I'd have drawn a total blank. But don't worry, I——'

'I'm not worrying. Don't kid yourself. But I must say

I did wonder why you looked so ghastly.' A note of faint concern rummaged through his voice. 'Porridge?'

'Mmm. . .' she murmured with an air of rueful distaste, 'and an orange if I really felt flush. My cat ate better than I did!'

'Well, you little idiot, why on earth didn't you ask me for something? I would have given you money. After all,' a wintry smile broke through his stern exterior, 'what is an unconventional husband for?'

'I couldn't. . .' she said quietly, lowering her eyes to an unravelling thread on the buttonhole of his shirt.

'Well, you couldn't have been that starving, then,' he began dismissively, preparing to rise.

'. . .because I don't know where you live.'

'Ah. . .That was clever of me!' he muttered, sitting down again. 'Here.' He withdrew a card from his breast pocket. 'That's where I live—but I don't suppose you need money now, do you? You have Julia Maudsby to run riot with.'

'Look,' she said suddenly, in some confusion, 'I didn't mean to sound as if I expected money from you. I wouldn't have dreamed of asking you, I just——'

'More fool you, then.' He looked at her for unfathomable seconds, leaving her eyes no choice but to stare into his. 'Glasses look good on you. They bring out that quirky amber colour of your eyes. Appropriate name—Jem.' His thoughts seemed to drift away and a blank look clouded his eyes momentarily. 'Right!' he suddenly said, making Jem jump. 'Back to the job in hand. What to do about your drawing? Now, look at it. It's not good enough,' and he made a couple of lightning strokes across Ida's trunk. Instantly the flat sketch took on roundness and life, a vitality and humour that drew reluctant admiration from Jem. No wonder his technique was lauded so fervently, she thought, even though the loftier critics had started giving him a rough time over an apparent surrender to commercialism in his latest works.

'Give her a bit more belly, fill her out. *She's* not anorexic. Feel her. . .Be her. . .Think fat.' He rose abruptly. 'It's all in the mind. Once you get inside the subject, take an excursion through their tissues and cavities, then you'll begin to know how it feels to be that person. Their idiosyncrasies of movement are revealed, the special tonal quality of muscle and skin. By the time you've finished drawing a person you should know them as intimately as you know yourself.'

'Well, in my sculpture——' Jem began unhappily.

'I'm not interested in your sculpture. I'm teaching form and anatomy, and yours could do with a great deal of help.' He eyed her dark green shift briefly, sending a rush of agonised colour to her cheeks. He seemed all too fond of sideways remarks about her appearance. She was not anorexic, just ill-fed, and she was acutely aware of how little it suited her. But it was not Darcy Lister's place to criticise her looks. Or was it. . .? Did a husband have those rights?

It was all too draining on her weakened metabolism. She sank down wearily.

'I'll keep all that in mind, Mr Lister,' she murmured. 'And I am going to work, I promise.'

'So I should hope,' he said curtly.

He was about to turn away when a thought occurred to him. 'Ah, yes. You asked me once, a long time ago, how you were going to repay me for the singular favour I'm doing you. Well, come to my house on Saturday. I'll show you! Eight a.m. sharp. I prefer the morning.'

Long after the clean, outdoor scent of him had been overpowered by turps and dust, Jem continued to ponder the pregnant meaning behind his words. What on earth could he want her for?

Still chewing it over, she made her way to the refectory. An aura of greasy chips called the faithful down the corridor to the holy shrine of fast food. Pilgrims jostled one another for a more advantageous position as the great doors opened, allowing them to pour in and assuage the pangs of starvation endured since breakfast.

Every one talked and no one listened to two and a half months' worth of holiday news. The first day of term was always loud.

Jem found her best friend, Yvonne Haverson, sitting in their usual corner.

'Hi, Jem!' plump, Mediterranean Yvonne called excitedly, making room. 'How's tricks?'

'Fine, fine,' Jem burbled. 'You look brown, Vonny.'

'So would you if you'd just come back from honeymoon in Skiathos!' Yvonne held out her left hand for admiration.

'Honeymoon? Oh, Vonny! You're married?'

Yvonne beamed. 'We made it all legal and binding four days before we went. And it wasn't half complicated trying to explain that the Miss Haverson on the passport was, in fact, the Mrs Westmoreland on the ticket.' She laughed loudly. 'But, oh, marriage is lovely. . .you should try it, Jem. Suddenly you feel all different. Important and self-satisfied and. . .and contented.'

'Do you?' Jem smiled sceptically at her friend and then recovered herself. 'I'm so happy for you, Vonny. I knew he'd win you round in the end.'

She listened attentively, laughing in all the right places as Yvonne described in graphic detail the wedding, the honeymoon, the problems involved in moving two flats into one, and the traumas of in-law visits, but all the time keeping a compartment of her brain ticking over with her own thoughts.

Could she, would she dare to confide *her* marriage to Yvonne? She longed to tell someone. The burden of the secret was heavy, and yet she knew her friend of old. Indiscretion was her middle name.

Watching her now, gabbling nineteen to the dozen, Jem decided against it. Not just yet, anyway. There would be plenty of time later if her British nationality thing took as long as the initial stages indicated. Could be anything up to two years, the Home Office had told her breezily. Ah, well, she was in no hurry.

Automatically she put the saucer over Yvonne's new husband Mike's cup of tea, resigned yet again to his non-appearance.

'What is it this time?' she asked.

'Oh, he's in the throes of inventing counterweighted furniture that either folds itself away into the ceiling when you don't need it, or into the floor. It's quite ingenious, but I think he's going to have to invent the house to go with it, too!'

'Like a Murphy bed, you mean?' Jem giggled, picturing Mr and Mrs Westmoreland's recumbent forms disappearing forever in a jangle of springs.

'Yes, but he's got tables, sideboards. . .cookers even, you name it. You know what he's like about space and clutter. Our flat's driving him barmy. There's not enough room to swing a cat. Speaking of cats, how's Ali, by the way?'

'Oh, he's fine,' Jem said, struggling to keep abreast

of her friend's mental agility. 'Still furious with me for keeping him in so much, but what else can I do? He'd make a tasty snack for the four horsemen of the Apocalypse down in the yard.'

'Who?' Even Yvonne seemed lost for words.

'The Alsatians the landlord keeps locked in the yard. They'd make mincemeat of poor Ali Cat.'

'Give him to me, then. He could have the run of our garden. Listen to that—"our". Doesn't it sound grand?'

Jem smiled, but shook her head. 'I couldn't. He's the only thing that's kept me sane these last three years. If it wasn't for his bumptious presence in that dark, miserable room I don't think I'd ever bother to go back there.'

'I don't know why you haven't moved ages ago,' said Yvonne feelingly.

'It's cheap,' was Jem's retort.

Yvonne raised her eyebrows and the subject was dropped. But later that night Ali himself vindicated Jem's deep faith in him by oozing round her legs, butting his great tabby head against the backs of her knees and chatting loquaciously about his day as her blunt tin-opener mashed up his cat-food tin. He was her cat, and her cat he would remain.

Saturday morning turned out cold and crisp. Cycling to Chiswick, where Darcy Lister lived, was going to take her ages, Jem decided, so she'd better set off at about six to ensure that she got there on time.

Finding something to wear had posed problems. Clothes tended to hang rather than drape since she'd become so skinny. It'll just have to be layers of bright colour to disguise the coat-hanger frame, she thought, and dug out some brilliant multi-coloured confections

in burnished copper and ultramarine, with a dash of
saffron for pep.

She smiled when she saw herself. 'Well, I glow if
nothing else. Here's to jumble sales and sari stalls!' She
gave her prehistoric treadle sewing-machine an affectionate pat on her way out.

Propping her bicycle against the gate-post of Darcy's
house in Bedford Park an hour and a half later, she
wandered down the front path of a large, detached,
pseudo-Dutch house. She'd rung the bell and was
standing back craning her neck to get a better view
when all of a sudden it struck her. 'Norman Shaw. . .of
course!' she said aloud, remembering the architect
from some long-past lecture. 'He designed Bedford
Park.'

'Well done! Go to the top of the class,' said a
mocking voice from behind her. As usual Mr Lister
had sprung up from nowhere, and Jem turned sharply
to find him striding up the garden path, a loaf of bread
and a paper under one arm and a stiff-legged white dog
of dubious ancestry bristling at his feet.

'You're early. Just in time for breakfast.' The dog
growled, unconvinced of her credentials. 'Hush,
Nathan. She's not selling religion, she's a
friend. . .Aren't you?' he added enquiringly as he
opened the front door and ushered her inside.

'You make some toast,' he commanded once they
were in the kitchen, 'while I make the tea and boil
some eggs. How do you like them? Three-minute or
bullet?'

'Soft, please,' she stammered, flicking nervous
glances here and there, hoping to spy a bread knife
without having to ask.

'It's in the drawer beside the sink.'

His conversational tone startled her. 'Oh, thanks,' she said. It seemed odd that he knew just what she was looking for. She sawed rather hopelessly at the loaf, knowing with dread the kind of mess she could make of it. As the mutilated slabs disintegrated beneath her hands she trembled with despair. How could she ever toast these?

The nervousness she'd suffered on the way to his house had been compounded a hundred-fold the instant he'd asked her to *cook* something. This will be inedible, she thought angrily, and it's all his fault. I hate cooking. I'm useless. Especially with an audience.

'In that case, I won't look,' came a bombshell from behind her.

Jem spun round and gawped at him, mouth wide open. How on earth could he know what she'd been thinking? Was he psychic? Did he indeed just materialise out of thin air by magic, as she had always suspected?

'Didn't you know you talk to yourself?' he asked mildly, seeing her astonishment. 'I've caught you at it frequently this week. It's been quite enlightening!'

A rosy blush crept across her cheekbones as she remembered some of the less than complimentary things she'd found herself thinking about him and his teaching methods. Arrogant, self-opinionated and cruel were samples of just the mildest. The realisation that he probably knew now what she thought of him was embarrassing beyond words.

'Oh, dear. I expect it's habit from talking to Ali all the time,' she muttered, trying to retrieve some honour out of chaos.

'And who the hell's Ali? Your house-boy?'

'My cat!' wailed Jem as the holey toast under the grill caught fire.

Quickly she whipped the grill-pan out and turned, intending to tip the flaming bread into the sink. The handle was red-hot, and with a shriek she flung the whole lot into the air and watched, horrified, as distress flares of burning toast arced through the kitchen, landing in smouldering piles on the quarry tiles.

Darcy stamped on most of them to extinguish any sullen, lingering flame and then silently handed her a dustpan and brush before cutting four more slices of bread.

'What do you do for an encore?' he asked with deceptive blandness as he tried to smash his way into a six-and-a-half-minute egg, "Coleslaw *flambé*?'

The food was consumed in an uneasy hush. Darcy appeared to be lost in his paper, but just occasionally she found his hard, clear eyes focusing on her with unblinking intensity. It was an uncomfortable feeling, and she was glad that her chronic astigmatism made it impossible for her to see him too clearly from across the table.

'Our first breakfast in wedded bliss has been a slight let-down, wouldn't you say? At least the tea was drinkable.'

A flush of distress rose to Jem's cheeks as she determinedly scrunched her way through the last blackened corner of crust. 'Look, I wish you wouldn't keep mentioning it.'

'What?'

'Well, you know. . .that we're married.'

'Why? Are you ashamed of me?'

'Of course not!' she said with some surprise. 'I just think, the more we say it out loud, the. . .the. . .' she floundered, catching herself in difficulties '. . .well, the more inevitable it seems.'

'What you mean is, if you hide your head in the sand it'll go away?'

She shrugged. 'Something like that.'

'What's so terrible about us being married? There's no love lost between us—or gained, for that matter—so what are you so squeamish about?'

'I just feel like an opportunist, that's all, and if people were ever to find out about it we'd. . .I'd look like a calculating minx.'

'Ah, so that's it. The "what will people think?" syndrome. I thought you were above that kind of influence. But, as it turns out that you're as suburban as the next person, we'll have to see what we can do. If you don't mention marriage, I'll try not to. How's that? Though I must confess, *I* find it quite stimulating living the undercover life. It gives me quite a thrill to see "my wife" sitting on her donkey in the life class, shoulders hunched, glasses tripping off the end of her nose, tongue clenched painfully between pearly teeth, and knowing that I'm the only person in on the secret!'

'You paint such a flattering picture,' Jem muttered, taken aback by his keen observation of her.

'All in a good cause, my dear. Come. It's time for me to take you upstairs and expose you to the horrors ahead.'

Her heart skipped several beats. 'Upstairs?' she croaked. 'What's upstairs?' A lurid scene of scarlet wall-hangings, ceiling mirrors and a giant leopardskin-covered bed flashed before her.

It is possible, she thought. Some of the most respect-able-seeming people have very shady alter egos. Per-haps I've got myself married to a sado-masochist, or——

His roar of laughter startled her. 'Nothing so dramatic, my dear. I'm taking you to my studio. I'm going to "do" you.'

Blushing furiously, she followed him up the stairs, squashily carpeted, soundproof; past a light, airy landing and then up again to emerge into a startlingly bright attic. The ceiling flew upwards to a peak above them, suspending vast skylights way out of reach that lit the whole room with clear, shadowless light.

She couldn't help a gasp of amazement at the scenes of disorder that met them.

'I know it's a mess, but don't touch a thing. *I* know where everything is and I like it like this.'

Cupboard doors hung open; a hugger-mugger of paint, canvas, and bits of a tree cluttered every available surface. Half-finished sketches were roughly impaled to the wall, overlapping and askew. A cup containing fossilised dregs added to the neglected air.

The table in the centre of the room had one short leg. . .or could it be three that were too long? Jem wondered as she leant cautiously on the edge and nearly sent all the turps cans and pencil shavings slithering to the floor.

'I told you not to touch anything,' came a cold, censorious warning.

An icicle of humiliation shot down her spine and she moved away, her brain racing. How quickly his mood changed, she pondered. How swiftly he turned from puss to panther.

With a curt nod he motioned her to sit. High and hard, the stool made her feel vulnerable and exposed, and the bleak, merciless light from the high windows focused on her like an interrogation lamp.

Three quarters of an hour later she felt as if she'd been through the Spanish Inquisition.

Looking angular and thoroughly unnatural, she sat, her chin resting in what was meant to be a winsome way, on her left shoulder, her eyes staring obliquely up towards the ceiling, and her head beginning to feel as if it had come unscrewed, with, all the while, Darcy's cold eyes penetrating her flesh.

What am I doing? she pondered to herself. This man scares me to death. The more I've seen of him, the less I want to, and yet here I am, trapped in this weird alliance. I should just stand up and leave.

But one glance at the dark, brooding brow convinced Jem to sit still and efface herself or risk provoking instant annihilation.

She marvelled at how he seemed to have the ability to slice through her fragile self-sufficiency, pull threads in her carefully woven security blanket, revealing the raw uncertainty of her loneliness deep inside. His piercing insight into her pretensions had been lent more impact by the calm, cruel way he used his words, often not in themselves so frightening, but given an extra bite by the flash of his teeth in a mirthless smile.

She reflected on how he seemed to seek her out during life class, apparently with the sole intention of causing her embarrassment, because the instant he had reduced her to a tongue-tied silence he would groan impatiently and walk away. She knew her life drawing, which had steadily improved under Caroline Mayhew, the previous artist lecturer, had taken a crashing dive into clumsy inflexibility with just a few ill-humoured words from the new incumbent. Now she knew she was going to have to block her mind to Mr Lister, or her art would suffer drastically.

Despite numerous breaks, the morning wore on. Darcy worked silently and with complete concentration. Jem marvelled at the speed with which he sketched, capturing the essence, tossing off a lightning flash of lines, then on to another page, another angle. Mere impressions, yet, from the glimpse she'd caught as one of the drawings had floated to the floor beside her, delicately perceptive.

Jem felt herself gradually relax in his preoccupied silence, and it wasn't until quite late in the afternoon that he stopped work. . .mainly because her stomach suddenly and inelegantly began to rumble.

'Enough!' he said, stretching languidly. 'You need sustenance, young woman.' And for the first time since Jem had met him, he smiled. A genuine, friendly grin that enlivened his eyes with humour and approachability.

And good looks, it dawned on her with a shock as she followed him downstairs.

An idea began in turbid embryo. The beginnings of it trembled loosely as she eyed him surreptitiously during the preparations of a scratch meal. By the time the table was laid and the soup heated through, Jem was quivering with suppressed excitement.

In the space of a few minutes the idea of sculpting Darcy Lister had become blind obsession. She had to do it.

Working out the ways and means left a dark frown across her brow, and she was startled into a squeak when suddenly she heard her name called, quite loudly.

'You haven't been listening to a word I've said, have you? What dark plot are you hatching?'

Guiltily she blushed. 'Sorry. I was thinking about

work.' No harm in stretching a point. 'What were you saying?'

He looked sceptical for a moment. 'That frown bodes ill for somebody, I'll be bound. It made you look like a very cross dove.'

'Jemima means "dove", so maybe that's why,' she blurted, glad to have a diversion. 'And Tortola, where I come from, means "turtle-dove" in Spanish. Isn't that strange?' She squirmed inwardly at her own mindlessness. Whatever had come over her?

He looked vaguely surprised, but refrained from eating her with intellectual superiority. 'Do you make a study of names? Mine's just the surname of my French great-grandfather, but I've no clue as to its meaning.' He laughed suddenly, a joyous sound that stirred an answering tickle in Jem's throat, 'But I think you and I have to thank a list-writing clerk for our surname, don't we? "Giles the lister, inventories a speciality".'

The tickle in Jem's throat changed to a tight constriction. 'Our surname.' Crazy though it seemed, she had forgotten again that she and he were inextricably tied. By a name. His.

'Mrs Lister.' She tried it out. 'Mrs Jemima Lister. It sounds so strange. Not me at all.' It was the first time she had really thought of it as her name, and her heart beat a little faster.

'Well, it is you. You can't escape it, so make the best of it while it lasts!'

Make the best of it? She couldn't imagine, apart from the grant, what possible 'best' there could be. And supposing something dreadful were to happen and she couldn't ever get free? Had to stay married to this frightening, intriguing man for the rest of her life? It didn't bear thinking about.

She jumped to her feet, collected her things about her in a sudden need to run away from the disturbing knowledge that she belonged to him, if only in name.

'What, going already?' he enquired with a hint of sarcasm.

'I have to. It's getting dark and it's a long way to Stoke Newington.' As she sidled past him at the door he caught her wrist, nearly wrapping his long, flexible fingers twice round its frailty.

'And as I was saying, which you so rudely ignored, wear something not quite so sacklike tomorrow. I'm going to try a bit more body.'

'Tomorrow!' Jem squeaked, appalled at the prospect of another eight hours of torture. 'I can't,' she lied. 'I'm doing something.'

'Well, undo it.' He spoke quietly, but his voice was overlaid with harshness, brooking no dissemble. 'You be here, or your friend, the garrulous Yvonne from Pottery, hears from the horse's mouth about our "arrangement". I've heard that it would then be a simple case of "light the blue touch-paper and stand back", and you wouldn't like that, would you Mrs Lister?'

She shrank away from him.

'Come on, now, I haven't tried to seduce you, have I? Heaven forbid! But you have an interesting face and I'm trying to capture the essence of it. Now. This week. Before that artistic, missionary zeal fades to mundanity.' His voice had become very low and earnest and he was bending slightly to focus on her startled eyes in the dusk. 'So come tomorrow and let me immortalise you.'

She could only nod, feeling the urgent grip of his

hand slacken and withdraw. She moved away down the garden path, faintly disturbed by the undertow of tension that had passed between them.

It rained heavily the next morning, so she was wet and tired when she arrived at his house, and dozed off twice during the morning's sitting. She jerked awake to find Nathan, the dog, lying beside her, eyebrow tufts a-jog, keeping a watching brief over her lest she molest his master. She tried smiling at him, but he flattened his ears suspiciously and scowled. She couldn't help a chuckle at the absurd solicitude he showed his large and capable master.

'Have you the temerity to laugh at my dog? He'll be mortally offended.' Darcy never paused in his swift portraiture, sweeping the page with exuberant curves of charcoal. Jem puzzled over how he managed to stay so clean.

'Mind you, he offends easily.' His eyes twinkled mischievously and Jem began to feel some of her perennial distrust evaporate at this obverse view of the usually taciturn Mr Lister. 'If I happen to give him some food he dislikes, he'll take the tin away and bury it in the garden. I think what he needs is a bit of competition.'

Jem smiled and was about to screw up her courage to make some contribution to this inconsequential chat when suddenly the door of the studio was rudely burst open and she heard the metallic clack of stiletto heels pounding across the wooden floor behind her.

'Ah, here you are, darling,' said a clipped, authoritative voice and a tall, elegant blonde hove into view. 'I've had a call from Max at the gallery. He wants to know when you plan to have that Retrospective you've promised him. He's getting himself in a tizzy.' She removed a pair of scarlet gloves and decided against putting them down on Darcy's paint table.

'Good morning, Venetia. How are you this dull Sunday?' Darcy muttered, not lifting his eyes from his work.

'Wet!' she said shortly, flicking imaginary raindrops from the sleeve of her scarlet coat. 'Get down, Nathan. I can't stand dog hairs.'

Jem, who to her relief, was being ignored, studied this new arrival. It was a grave mistake, she thought, for a woman to bleach her hair to that particular stridency and then wear bright red, particularly as she had such pale, fine skin. And perhaps her eyes and lips seemed so icy because of the unsympathetic choice of make-up. Pale blue shadow and a thin slash of Jezebel were not exactly subtle.

Darcy looked up at that moment and caught her eyeing the 'Scarlet Woman', as she'd already dubbed her.

'Ah, Venetia, let me introduce you to my. . .' He paused infinitesimally, enjoying himself as he saw Jem stiffen, 'my new model, Jemima Selby. Jemima, Venetia Pitt, my agent, guide and mentor.'

Venetia gave Jem's shy smile a cursory glance and then turned her attention back to what interested her most, trying a little more saccharin this time to get what she wanted from him.

'Darcy, darling; you know Max won't make a groat out of this exhibition. He's only doing it because he admires your work *so* much. The least you can do is show some interest and lend him a few paintings.'

Darcy laid down his charcoal with exaggerated casualness, a gesture that would have had Jem quaking if aimed in her direction. 'Dear Max. So altruistic. Such a selfless lover of fine art. Who is he trying to kid, Venetia? Not you, surely, my shrewd, foxy lady? You know as well as I do, he'll have one of his raving loony Art Speak thrashes going on downstairs through which my faithful fans will have to fight their way to reach my modest offering above. He'll make money hand over fist on the avant-garde junk sales with my non-profit-making name to draw the crowds. The only person guaranteed not to make a sou will be me.'

'Now, now, my cynical baby,' she murmured, trailing a blood-red nail across his cheek. 'You're being grand again, and you know how your little Venetia gets fwikened when you're so forceful.'

Jem turned her face away. The sight of Venetia Pitt, so tall and cool and self-assured, draping herself around Darcy filled her with an inexplicable distaste. And the lithping little-girl act. Nauseating. Surely he could see through it? Or perhaps, she thought critically, he preferred not to. Perhaps he was one of those men who liked their women simpering and obviously insincere.

A hush tightened around her. A vibrant, poisonous hush. She sprang up, a hand across her mouth. She knew the instant she looked into the eyes of the woman opposite what she'd done. She'd spoken those disparaging, undeniably rude thoughts of hers out loud, in a voice as clear as crystal.

'That's a trick that's going to get you into serious trouble, Miss Selby. Take care what thoughts you think before you start broadcasting them to the world.'

But it wasn't Darcy who frightened her this time. It was the toe-curling look of malevolent hatred that shot across the room and lodged an inch above her heart that made her break out in a sweat of fear. Fear of Venetia Pitt.

CHAPTER FOUR

'BUT I did apologise,' Jem muttered defensively, aware of how sulky she must sound. 'I told her that my tongue tends to run away with my thoughts, even though I don't intend it to.'

'That's no consolation to Venetia, is it?' Darcy was busy setting up another pose, defusing the aftermath of a traumatic disturbance. 'Aloud or silent, she now knows in no uncertain terms just what you think of her. She's every right to be furious.'

'Yes.' Jem paused, suddenly feeling the need to have his sympathy. 'I never felt so terrible in my life as when I saw her face,' she said as he pushed her into a chair, 'and I realised what a dreadful thing I'd done. I thought she was going to kill me.'

She failed with the sympathy. 'Not outright,' Darcy drawled sardonically. 'Venetia prefers the long-drawn-out technique!'

'Oh, she definitely hates me now.'

She shuddered convulsively, remembering the snakelike quality with which Venetia had slithered across the room towards her. The pale almond eyes that her pierced her with a long, drilling stare before she had been reduced to a quivering wreck with just four apocalyptically ominous words. 'I shall remember you!'

'Oh, how could I have been so foolish? So unguarded? I *know* I talk to myself, and I do try to curb the habit. But why, oh, why did I have to lapse

45

then, of all times? I've made an implacable enemy now.' And the worst thing was that she would be forever running into that enemy as they both trotted in and out of Darcy's life like Rain and Shine in a weather house.

Darcy cast her an exasperated look. 'Stop getting so agitated. I'm trying to draw your ear, dammit!' Obviously she would get no help from him!

Oh, Grandma, she thought suddenly, careful not to shape it into words, what have I done? How can I get myself out of this mess? She realised she was alone, isolated in this marriage of deception that she and this stranger were indulging in. The knowledge was like a cage clanging shut on her freedom. She was trapped with no one to talk to. . .and her grandmother was three thousand miles away.

She was brought sharply out of her self-pity by a hat. Old and straw and prickly as it rested on her ears.

'Don't move an eyelash,' Darcy muttered, 'or that thing will fall down to your chin.'

All the while he worked, concentration intensifying the severity of his good looks, Jem, with head rigidly still, churned over the disaster of the morning. Unconsciously she shifted in her chair to try to banish such morbid thoughts, and immediately regretted it as she felt the hat slowly obliterate her face.

Instantly afraid of Darcy's sudden wrath, she lifted the brim and blinked at him tentatively, like a baby owl caught in a torch beam.

'Sorry!' she whispered.

Vaguely she became aware that he had left his easel and was walking, with great deliberation, towards her, an unreadable expression on his face. Frantically she juggled with the hat, knowing that his bland features could be hiding a blast furnace of explosive anger, or worse, a cold, sneering sarcasm from whose lethal annihilation she cringed even more.

He loomed over her, handsomely domineering. Light from the window glinted on his startling hair, catching his high cheekbones and the smooth, clean lines of his jaw as he stared down at her, daring her with a lift of his black brow to look away.

Captured, like one of Dr Mesmer's victims, all she could do was pray that, whatever her nemesis, it was swift.

'Poor little goose. The dreaded Venetia has really shaken you, hasn't she?'

Relief flooded through Jem as she saw his expression of stern dispassion take on the mellower tones of sympathy. She couldn't help it. Her sudden shift of emotions caught her off balance and dissolved her into tears.

'I'm scared. What will she do to me?' she managed to splutter between sobs, with her head in her hands and the hat at a rakish angle.

'I wouldn't let her harm you,' Darcy said evenly, and there seemed to be a meaning in the timbre of his voice beyond the mere words.

'You couldn't stop her. She's not going to ask your permission, even if she does think she's in love with you——'

'Oh, she does, does she?' he broke in, apparently amused by this bold burst of feminine insight. 'But you think she's deluding herself?'

Startled by her own forthrightness, but defiant nevertheless, Jem battled on. 'Well, she wants something from you, anyone can see that. But it looks like habit to me. As if she's been thinking about it for so long, she believes her own propaganda. . .Oh, dear, have I upset you——?' She broke off in alarm as Darcy ran his hand quickly over his face to hide the smile that threatened his gravity.

'You're quite an authority on "The Pitts", even after such a short acquaintance! How do you do it? I dread to think what character assassination *I've* suffered at your hand since we met.'

'I'm sorry. I wasn't meaning to be offensive. I just thought, being so close to her, you might not notice these things.'

'Am I close to Venetia?'

'I don't know, but I think she would like to think you are.' Bitterly regretting her foolish interference, Jem groped in her basket for a plaster-encrusted hanky, endeavouring to dry her face on what felt like a reject from the London brickworks.

Surreptitiously she studied his face. She was puzzled by her own bravery, but after the débâcle with Venetia Pitt to be timid and self-effacing seemed absurd. Hiding behind her own supposed anonymity served no good purpose. She might as well give herself cause to be frightened of him by speaking her mind rather than staying silent and fearing him anyway.

Suddenly he was squatting on his haunches, one arm resting on the back of her chair, and when he next spoke he was close enough for her to feel his breath.

'Have you ever been in love, little Jem?'

Surprised though she was, she was beginning to get used to Darcy's unconventional questions. 'No,' she replied, a little unsteadily. 'Why?'

'Just curious. I was trying to imagine how you would go about it.' He smiled a slow, ambiguous smile. 'Jump in with both feet and wade through it with the same whole-heartedness you apply to everything, I should think. It should be quite some sight to see!'

'I shan't be making myself into a spectator sport,' Jem replied tartly, 'because I've no intention of falling in love. Not until I get my degree and am completely independent. I haven't got the time, and it's too distracting.'

'So, there's no room in your order of events for being swept off your feet? I'm very impressed by your self-control, I must say. To know that your heart couldn't be overturned by anything unexpected.'

'Nothing is unexpected if you guard against it,' she said, rather piously.

'Really?' he murmured. 'How about this?' And with a movement like molten silver he encircled her with his arms and covered her half-open lips with the startlingly sensual warmth of his.

Frozen with shock, Jem stiffened as his mouth began to move rhythmically and his hands to explore the embarrassingly hollow hollows of her back. A reluctant tingle began on her scalp, trickling downwards until it reached her stomach, where it spread warmly like golden syrup over a pudding, making her tense limbs melt and her eyelids flutter dreamily closed.

She had never felt anything like the bitter-sweet sensation as his lips caressed, just moist, slightly slippery, wholly drugging to the senses. And, just as she was beginning to feel her consciousness opening out like a June rose, all too brief.

Abruptly he pulled away. 'There were two things you should have guarded against there. Firstly, my predatory instincts, and secondly, your treacherously warm ones. You were really enjoying that towards the end, weren't you?'

Somewhat befuddled by this brief glimpse into the murky world of the physical, Jem tried to defend herself. 'You're obviously well versed in the art of seduction.'

'Oh, I've had a bit of practice! But surely you can't be as completely innocent as you seem? Not at—how old? Twenty-one?'

Jem thought it safest to remain silent on that score. Apart from anything else, a severe case of reaction was setting in, and she could feel her stomach quivering in a most disturbing fashion as she recalled the touch of his lips. Perhaps her voice would quiver, too.

Of course she'd been kissed before, but the difference between the immature fumbles snatched in the stroboscopic darkness of the college dance-floor and what she had just tasted was too colossal to believe. Darcy's kiss had made her realise that somewhere along the line in her well-ordered, sentiment-free existence she had been missing out.

A strange devil-may-care feeling rose, unbidden, to her throat, and for a perilous moment she felt almost compelled to sing.

With a start she brought herself back to earth. He was still on one knee beside her, his warm hand cupped beneath her elbow, sky-blue eyes crinkled round the edges as he smiled at her with a quiet mockery which she found difficulty taking offence at.

'You haven't answered my question yet, you secretive little creature. Is this reticence purely a smokescreen?'

Meeting his gaze with a new, exhilarating boldness, she took a deep breath. 'Wouldn't you like to know?' she heard herself say with the flirtatious lilt of a soap-opera queen and watched, with a sharp pang of embarrassed disappointment, as he rose and turned away.

'No, my sweet, I wouldn't.' He gave her a regretful look. 'You mustn't throw down challenges you're too inexperienced to follow through, because one of these days you'll come up against someone who hasn't got as many scruples as I have.'

Jem felt a blush suffuse her face, and he relented a little in his lecturing tone. 'I wouldn't want to find out from you anyway, Jem Lister, because I make it a rule never to seduce a married woman!'

By the time she had reached home that night Jem had convinced herself that Darcy Lister must think her a fool and an unmitigated harlot. By constantly reiterating to herself that one, mildy suggestive remark, she had blown it up out of all proportion. Now it seemed outrageously smutty and vaguely unpleasant.

She imagined she saw the look of distaste on his face as he had turned disgustedly away, and no amount of rational argument, put forward by the tiny part of her that retained some sense, could dissuade the irrational majority from flying off into the realms of despair.

What she felt the next day when, during 'refec', she learned from Yvonne, the cyes and cars of the world, that Darcy Lister's reputation had gone before him, was anything but embarrassment.

'He's had more girls than you could count on the fingers of the Eighth Army,' Yvonne hissed conspiratorially as Jem guardedly watched the subject under discussion at the far end of the room. He was leaning familiarly over a well-endowed, vivacious blonde, one arm across the back of her chair, the other resting on the table just beside her upthrust breasts.

An animated conversation proceeded for a moment before he took her earlobe between his finger and thumb and jiggled her head with an affectionate tug.

'That's number four since last Monday,' came Yvonne's sepulchral tones as the girl rose to follow Darcy out of the canteen, swinging her tightly clad hips in triumph. 'He's insatiable!'

Jem tried not to show how riveted she was, but she felt her gaze lingering on his back as he pushed open the heavy door and stood aside to allow the young woman to precede him.

'How do you know all this?' she ventured when the last gleam of silver hair had vanished in the gloom of the corridor. 'He's only just started here.'

'Ah, but news travels when you know which flight-path it's on!' Yvonne lowered her voice conspiratorially. 'He *says* it's for modelling, but really it's an excuse to get them back to his house, and. . .well, you can guess what happens. I don't expect he gets much painting done!'

It had been difficult, as Jem confided in Ali that night, not to rise there and then and beat a tattoo on the Formica. 'There had I been suffering untold agonies over my ineffectual stab at a "come-on", when all the time he and his various mistresses make public assignations, blatant, pulsing with suggestion. How dare he be so patronising to me when all the time he's taking his pick of the most notoriously accommodating girls in the whole college?'

She stamped around her room, barking her shins on the claustrophobic furniture. It was a relief, in a way, to lose her feelings of guilt, but there lurked in the depths of her self-esteem a niggling humiliation that she obviously possessed so little allure that he'd had no difficulty in rebuffing her.

As Ali blinked owlishly from his vantage-point on the bed, a slow dejection slunk between the cracks of her self-righteous anger. Gradually her shoulders drooped and she slumped down next to the cat, the bouncing bantam-cock knocked out of her by a seeping self-pity. Life had been so simple before Darcy Lister had thrust his assertive presence under her nose. Now it seemed that at every corner she bumped into another aspect of his forceful influence. She just couldn't escape him.

Ali pushed his great plate face into hers as a pick-me-up for jaded spirits. Jem fondled him distractedly, smiling despite herself. 'You old bum!' she murmured rudely. 'You're right, I will snap out of it. Far from letting him get me down, I'll show him just what a ball of fire I can be. He'll see!'

This new determination carried her through the rest of the week. Instead of feebly submitting to Darcy's scathing comments about her life drawing, she began to challenge him.

'Perhaps, Mr Lister, this method of destroying a pupil in order to build her up again in your own image works in most cases. In mine it doesn't. . .so I would appreciate it if you would give me constructive criticism, not annihilation.' She had the sweet satisfaction of seeing him almost lost for words and pushed home her advantage. 'I attend your classes in order to learn about the human body; all you've taught me so far is how to duck brickbats, but that won't help me to become a better sculptor.'

'As the name implies, Miss Selby, I aim to teach "Life", whether anatomical or metaphysical. I naturally assumed you would appreciate a grounding in both.'

The colossal conceit of the man left Jem temporarily speechless, though seething with a new flood of angry adrenalin. I will. . .I'll show him. . .she vowed silently, fumbling the two jagged halves of a pencil into the folds of her skirt in order to conceal the fact that she'd just snapped it in her fury.

As a test of her immature assertiveness she decided that that very day she would begin on the preliminary drawings for the sculpture she was going to do of her new-found adversary. The only trouble was. . .he wouldn't keep still.

Bending, squatting, leaning languidly against a chair, passing some derogatory comment—all were accomplished with the minimum of apparent effort but were, nevertheless, a constant flow of movement. By the end of half an hour Jem's paper resembled a chimpanzee's attempt at the roof of the Sistine Chapel.

Doggedly she stuck at it, knowing that she had to grasp the dominant line of each pose as quickly as possible in order to capture his loose-limbed freedom of movement. Her excitement mounted as she recognised the power taking shape in the crude, hasty lines. She felt an element almost of mysticism creeping into the work as form and purpose appeared between the lines that she had no idea she had intended or was capable of.

The morning passed in a haze. She was only distantly aware of the hall clock chiming or of sporadic movement and gentle bursts of conversation. She was immersed.

Just before lunch-break Darcy stretched lazily and hauled his sweater on, instantly clarifying for Jem something that had long been niggling. His clothes!

'Oh, what's he doing putting clothes *on*?' she muttered indistinctly. 'He should be taking them off. . .only so I can understand how he hangs together,' she added hastily to save her own blushes, 'and see if the tonal quality of his muscles is as well defined as I imagine, even though he is so slim and agile.' A faint chuckle escaped her as she imagined his face if she asked him to strip. It would be worth a guinea a box.

The rest of the day passed quickly. At the least sign of Darcy heading in her direction she would dash off a hasty likeness of fat Ida, patiently recumbent on her chaise-longue, using her new, speedy technique, and was mollified to receive words of encouragement. Then, the instant he had turned his back, her eyes followed him and her pencil recorded his every move. By the time the mid-autumn dusk had reached into the corners of the studio, Jem knew that this was the best work she had ever done.

In the pre-dawn gloom of the following Saturday she blearily set off again on the Chiswickward trek.

She had plenty of time to think as she laboriously pedalled the miles to Darcy's house, and it struck her how odd it was that he never allowed her to see any of his work. There were lots of large canvasses stacked around the studio, but all of them faced the wall. There were no working drawings on display, no watercolours, nothing. . .only the unfinished charcoal sketches of her. He seemed remarkably reticent about his work.

She knew his style from books and exhibitions she'd been to. Definitely representational, though flamboyant and wild, with an exaggerated use of colour. His subject was usually figures, deceptively simple yet always revealing, on closer examination, complicated allegories of black humour or bathos. A difficult painter to understand, she reflected. . .just as difficult as was the man.

Jem sighed. I like his work, she thought, but its

complexities must mirror his inner, sardonic view of life. That's quite a frightening prospect!

Quite suddenly, as she rounded a sharp left-hand bend, her reflections were brought to a singularly spectacular halt.

The door of the parked car she was passing was flung open in her face, swiping her neatly off her bicycle and landing her in a heap in the middle of the road.

Two seconds later the bike landed on top of her.

'What the hell happened to you?' was Darcy's welcoming greeting as she limped up the garden path, two and a half hours late. 'What's happened to your face?'

He reached out and gently touched her grazed cheek, a look of concern crossing his face as she flinched away from him.

'I had an argument with a car,' she said lightly, not wishing to play on his sympathies. 'I'm all right.'

'Yes, I can see you are,' he muttered drily as he took her elbow and eased her into a chair. 'Why ever did you come? Why didn't you ring and call it off?'

'The driver of the car gave me a lift to Green Park tube station. It didn't seem so far when I set off. . .' She trailed off, exhausted and in pain.

'Have you seen a doctor? You look terrible.'

'Thanks! And no, I haven't. There's nothing broken. On me, that is. My bike's a write-off.'

'Bike!' he exploded. 'Don't tell me you were riding a bicycle from. . .what the hell's the name of that back of beyond where you live? Islington? Paddington?'

'Stoke Newington, and yes, I was. How else do you think I get about? It would cost me half my grant to use the tube.'

He stared at her, speechless for a moment. 'Do you mean to say that I've let you cycle home all that way in the dark? I should be shot.' He ran his hand distractedly through his hair before noticing the raw grazes across the back of her hand and her tattered stockings.

'Oh, you poor girl,' he murmured, squatting down beside her. 'How on earth did it happen?'

Jem hesitantly told him what bits she could remember; of what felt like the north face of the Eiger leaping into her path; of coming to in the road with a set of headlights bearing down on her; of the miraculous escape she'd had when the driver saw her just in time, and of the distraught lady who had been in the parked car, and who then drove her to the tube, explaining that if her husband found out where she'd been he would kill her because he'd think she'd been with a manfriend, which of course she hadn't, so would Jem *please* not tell the police or she would be done for.

Darcy listened with a set expression on his face.

'You *did* tell the police. . .didn't you?'

'No. . .how could I? I didn't want to get her into trouble.'

'And, of course, you didn't take her number?'

'No.' She felt resentment well up in her as he bombarded her with these questions. What business was it of his? Couldn't he see how ill she felt? Her head ached and the whole of her right side felt tenderised.

'I think I'd better go home and have a rest,' she murmured, rising unsteadily to her feet. 'I'm afraid I feel a bit peculiar.' And as he moved forward to help her she collapsed in a crumple of second-hand Liberty print at his feet.

CHAPTER FIVE

DARCY'S doctor sent Jem to bed for three days.

'I'm all right, really I am,' she protested, drawing the breeze-scented sheets round her chin to prevent Darcy catching a glimpse of her neck peeping out of his own pyjama top. 'I'm quite well enough to go home.'

'Off you go!' he taunted callously, knowing her legs wouldn't carry her even as far as the corner shop. 'You can take Nathan for a nice long walk while you're at it.'

'Oh, please. . .you don't understand,' she wailed querulously. 'I've got to get back by tonight. Ali can't survive on his own.'

'Ali. . .? Oh, Ali, the feline house-boy. Well, couldn't you ring and get someone to feed him for you?'

'I don't know anyone that well.' She was beginning to get agitated and Darcy noted with slight concern the two spots of bright pink that had begun to glow on her pallid cheeks.

'Give me your key,' he sighed resignedly. 'I'll go and feed the brute. But if I have any trouble with him,' he added heartlessly, 'he'll have to fend for himself.'

After he'd gone Jem lay and pondered, not convinced that he wouldn't carry out his threat. 'And knowing Ali's reaction to strangers, he might have good cause!' she murmured, trying to erase the distressing vision of a rain-sodden tabby tom abandoned beside some noisome dustbin as she fell into disjointed sleep.

The first thing she saw when she opened her eyes a good three hours later was Ali's startled face peering at her, inches from her nose. 'Oh, Ali! Thank goodness! I was just picturing you in *Breakfast at Tiffany's*,' she croaked, lifting a weak hand to fondle his ear. 'Did Darcy bring you?'

'Yes, I did, and I'm beginning to wish I hadn't. He's already beaten up Nathan.' The state of Darcy's temper was manifestly evident, and waves of insecurity lapped around her as she struggled in vain to focus on the source of his irritable voice.

'Thank you so much for bringing him here,' she whispered placatingly. 'You're very kind.'

'I'm not the slightest bit kind,' he growled. 'I've brought him here to save myself that dreadful journey every day. I can't believe you did it on a bike. You must have been mad.'

'It was you who insisted.' She felt she had to set the record straight. She didn't fancy being accused of insanity.

'True,' he conceded. 'I'll have to organise something better in future.' He took a couple of strides towards the bed, suddenly leaping into sharp focus. Jem was horrified to see blood trickling, in an incongruously dainty rivulet, down his cheek.

'You've been hurt!' she gasped, instinctively reaching out a hand to touch his face. 'What have you done?'

'A slight altercation with Puss-in-Boots there. We had a clash of wills. Mine, needless to say, triumphed.'

Jem tried very hard to hide a smile. Ali was a wily old bird but his final resort, when doomed to capture, was to come out fighting.

'He does pack quite a punch, doesn't he? Now you know why I call him Mohammed Ali Cat!'

A look of disbelief burst through Darcy's thunderous expression, and then suddenly a great peal of laughter ricocheted round the bedroom.

Although it made her jump out of her skin, Jem found his laughter irresistibly infectious. A giggle escaped her, and as their eyes met they both found that their laughter was self-perpetuating, fuelled by a sudden mutual appreciation. 'Only you could dream up an absurd name like that,' he laughed, going off into fresh paroxysms.

Even while she was doubled up with laughter Jem's professional streak noted the pleasant creases that past laughter had left down his smooth brown cheeks; his even white teeth; the strong muscles in his neck as he threw back his head in an unconscious gesture of blithe gusto. She was sublimely ignorant of the elfin beauty gradually blossoming on her own face, enlivened by her cheeky grin, but the sudden sting as salt tears of laughter bit into her grazes made her wince, and a look of baffled pain shut off her spontaneity like a tap.

Gently Darcy dabbed at the tears with his handkerchief, carefully avoiding any cuts. With his free hand under her chin, he turned her face to the light. With a strange, languorous excitement, Jem felt the tips of his fingers brush the bloom of her cheek, so lightly as to be barely discernible, and her ears began to pound as his stern lips softened and his head slowly moved closer to hers. . .

'What a touching little scene!' The icicles in the high, clear voice shattered the stillness. Darcy turned, obliterating the person in the doorway, but Jem didn't need to see her to suppose that Venetia Pitt was in the kind of mood for tearing telephone directories in half.

A tight smile edged across Venetia's lips as she moved into the room. Jem realised that the pale blue eyes, hooded yet as sharp as gimlets, had missed not one iota of the undertows passing so briefly between Darcy and herself. She managed to shift to the far limits of the single bed without actually falling out and waited, trembling, for the explosion that she knew would follow.

'Darcy, darling, you ought to be more careful.' The sugar-sweet archness took Jem aback. 'What have you been doing to her? The poor child looks awful!'

Jem flinched as an eagle's talon swooped towards her face and she felt the fingers of Venetia's cold hand replace Darcy's warm, sensitive touch. She sensed her eyes begin to water as she felt the long nails dig in and, with minute exactitude, squeeze the half-ripe bruise on her cheek just a fraction too hard.

Darcy rose from the side of the bed and moved away. 'I should imagine she *feels* awful, too,' he said ungallantly. 'But she brought it on herself. She ought to know better at her age than to ride a bicycle through London in the dark. Some idiot knocked her off.'

'Oh, the poor thing!' Venetia's sympathy was like cod-liver oil—it left a nasty taste in the mouth. 'But I'm sure you'll make sure she gets better and is up and about in no time. Won't you, my dear?' Jem thought she made it sound like a threat, but Darcy just gave her his saturnine smile and seemed not to notice.

'How old is she, anyway?' Venetia suddenly asked, making Jem feel like a piece of horseflesh at auction. 'Surely no more than twenty? Straight out of school, my dear. A mere juvenile.'

'Yes, I have to admit she makes me feel positively antique. She's so passionate about everything.'

Venetia's smile slipped only fractionally. 'I *think* I know what you mean. All that *Angst* can wear you down after a while, can't it? I have to admit, getting slightly older does have its rewards.' She gave a side-long glance at Jem's flushed disarray as she lovingly preened herself in the wardrobe mirror. 'Tell you what, darling,' she continued, not taking her eyes off her image in the glass, 'if you get me a nice, cold Martini I'll take you out to lunch.'

'All right,' he said, moving smoothly towards the door. 'But it's my treat today. Expense-account lunches give me heartburn.'

'Oh, I insist. This time I'll put the company cheque-book away. Lunch is on me.'

Jem watched them, comfortable adversaries in a long-standing game, and felt the loneliness of exclusion settle over her.

'In that case,' he said with a grin, 'I'll allow the salmon mousse to give me chronic indigestion, and I won't mind a bit.'

Jem watched forlornly as Venetia linked her arm through Darcy's and headed for the door.

It's as if they've forgotten I exist, she thought, aware suddenly that Darcy hadn't even said goodbye.

It had all been so smooth, she realised. . .so adeptly done. With hardly a flicker Venetia had manoeuvred Darcy out of the room, jollying him into a receptive mood while simultaneously deriding Jem in an oh, so 'caring' way. That was just to prove to her, Jem supposed, how tightly Darcy was twisted round Venetia's little finger.

Jem felt lumpish and distinctly unattractive as she

subsided on to the pillow, forcing the memory of the brief, molten look in Darcy's eyes way into the back of her mind.

Ali hauled himself out from under the bed, crawling on his stomach in case he was attacked by sharp voices.

'You coward!' Jem called quietly. 'Fat lot of support you gave me. . .Still, roll on the day after tomorrow. We'll be out of this place so fast our feet won't touch the ground.'

But, after two days alternately resting and fidgeting, hearing first the bustle of Darcy's 'daily' followed by the breathless giggles of at least three young females as they, separately, made the pilgrimage past her door to a sitting with Darcy in his studio, Jem went down to the kitchen on the third morning to be greeted by a bombshell.

'I've decided that you will have to come and live here with me.'

After a few seconds of numb shock Jem launched a protest.

'I will not!'

'I've decided, and yes, you will!'

'You can't dictate to me like this.'

'Try me!'

She tried another tack. 'Why should you want me here? What possible reason can you have?'

'There are several. One of which is that now I know about that journey, I'm not going to have that on my conscience any more.'

'Oh, if that's all, then, there's a simple answer. I'll stop coming here.'

'Oh, no, you won't. Not if you want our marriage kept out of the tabloid gossip columns, Mrs Lister.'

'Don't keep calling me that. It's blackmail!'

'Yes,' he muttered simply, handing her the tea he'd automatically poured when she had finished her first cup.

'I won't come.' She could feel panic welling up in her as she watched his cool detachment. 'I hate this house!'

'Really?' His voice sounded like the silky purr of a tiger as it played with its prey. 'It's up to you, of course, but I would think that anything's better than that dreary dump you've been living in. It depressed the hell out of me, and I was only there for two seconds. What can you possibly hate about this house in comparison?'

Jem was trapped and she knew it. How could she confess to the fear and distrust, the confusion, the total inadequacies that piled in on her the moment the door closed and she was alone in his company? 'I just don't like it,' she muttered weakly, feeling again his personality crushing her will. 'I wouldn't be happy here.'

'Who said anything about being happy?' he snorted. 'It's convenient. It's practical. It suits me and, with a bit of effort, you could make it suit you. I'm not advocating this as a rest cure. It's work, pure and simple. . .for both of us. If you like, you get your own studio thrown in.' This was added almost as an after-thought, and Jem wasn't sure if she'd heard him correctly until he added, 'The conservatory's spare. You can have that.' And, as if that clinched it, he returned to his paper dismissively.

A studio. All to herself. Room to experiment! Space in which to make a mess without compunction! Suddenly, living in Darcy's house didn't seem quite so unspeakable.

She had to admit to feelings of opportunism, but

surely she couldn't refuse such a wonderful chance just for the sake of squeamishness? She was still horribly aware of the pitfalls of living in the same house as Darcy, and she was annoyed at finding herself capitulating with barely a fight. But at least he doesn't know what a pushover I am, she thought.

Or did he?

'Right, then,' he said decisively, folding his paper with a crackle. 'We'll collect your gear at the weekend.'

'I haven't said I'm coming yet,' she said peevishly, feeling cornered by his brio. 'I've got to have time to think about it.' Time to step back and ponder on the effect his daily presence would have on her. It was going to be difficult. Could she cope? she wondered. Maybe it was just because of her accident that she felt unusually weak-willed this morning, but whatever, she was going to have to steel herself against his determined take-over. When she came to live here it was to be on her terms. . .not his.

'No need,' he said offhandedly as he filled the dishwasher with practised nonchalance. 'I've done all the thinking that has to be done. All you have to do is pack.'

Well, she thought, so much for self-determination! He's won hands down this time.

Four days later she was in, lock, stock and cat.

It turned out to be not as hellish as she'd feared. In fact, barring breakfast and the occasional dinner together when he happened to be at home, she rarely saw him on the days he didn't teach.

She heard him, though—singing with off-key bravura in the bathroom, or earnestly taking the mickey out of an adoring Nathan in the large, unkempt garden.

And she felt his predominance everywhere. In the

eclectic mix of modern, Italian designer furniture and refurbished junk-shop treasures. The paintings and prints that flowed in a 'Who's Who of Art' around the walls. 'Swaps,' he said, indicating a couple of early Hockneys and a Francis Bacon. 'Dave gave mine away!'

It seemed strange, knowing that when she left the sanctuary of her light and airy bedroom she was vulnerable to the whim of his sudden appearance, but she got so used to the idea as to be almost unconcerned when they bumped in the bathroom doorway, or when they both ran to answer the phone at the same moment. Almost. . .but not quite!

She was collecting twigs and long-dead flowers to decorate her studio one evening when he strolled towards her across the lawn. 'You seem to be settling in reasonably well.' His hair shone eerily in the dusk. 'Not hating the place quite so much?'

She straightened, clutching her prickly bouquet to her bosom defensively. 'Yes. . .no. . .'

'At least it's better than the ghetto you were in.'

'I suppose so,' she said, not sure if he expected fawning gratitude. 'At least Ali can go out into the garden whenever he wants.'

'Is that all my selfless generosity means to you?' he groaned. 'An earth closet for your damned cat?'

She couldn't help laughing. 'Oh. . .and limitless baths and being warm and having my own studio. That most of all.' Her amber eyes glowed. 'It's wonderful having the space. I've brought all my work home from college, yet there's still masses of room.'

'I hate to say I told you so.' He paused and she got the impression that this conversation was not as casual as she'd first supposed. His next comment confirmed it.

'Er. . .how's Venetia treating you these days? Has she resumed hostilities?'

Jem's stomach bunched painfully at the mention of that name. 'How do you mean?' she began cautiously, aware of the narrow path she was treading. 'I tend to keep out of her way if I can.' She forgave the exaggeration of her own euphemism for hiding abjectly in her room whenever the strident tones of Venetia were heard. 'Why? Have you told her. . .you know. . .about us being. . .married?'

She felt the flashing blue of his eyes in the gathering gloom. 'Good lord, no. She's thoroughly enjoying disliking you. I wouldn't want to spoil her fun.'

Jem took a lurching breath. 'Well, you're going to have to tell her. You can't lie to her like this.' She wondered why she was being so self-sacrificing when she knew only too well that the Scarlet Woman would hate her twice as vehemently once she knew the true state of affairs.

'I'll leave that up to you, if you feel so strongly about it. Perhaps you'll get your chance at Christmas.'

'Christmas?' croaked Jem. 'What about Christmas?'

'Well, if you're intending to stay here. . .'

'I was, yes, if that's all right.'

'That's fine. You and Venetia can have a pleasant time together!'

Jem threw her gleanings down on to a weathered garden bench. 'Whatever are you being so devious about, Darcy? Tell me before I. . .' Words failed her.

'I just thought I'd better warn you that Ms Pitt has offered to house-sit over Christmas while I'm with my family in Herefordshire. I assumed you wouldn't want to make it *à deux*.'

A sudden bleakness opened up before her. 'No. . .no, I certainly wouldn't. But why didn't you ask me? I would have looked after the house. I. . .never do anything at Christmas, anyway.'

'Venetia asked first. I suspect it's to make sure that you don't have any all-night rave-ups.'

'Oh!' There didn't seem to be anything else to say.

'So, what are you going to do instead?'

A deep, resentful anger began to well up into her throat. 'You should tell *me*. You're the one who appears to rule my life for me. I was perfectly happy till you came along and started interfering in——'

'Jem Lister!' he interrupted sharply. 'May the Lord strike a hump on your back! You were the most insecure, miserable scrap of humanity before I got hold of you. There's been nothing but glowing improvement since the day we met. Admit it!'

'But you treat me like——'

'Admit it!' He took hold of her shoulders, playfully shaking her.

The truth in what he said gradually began to dispel the useless affront she had felt at his arrogance. 'I plead the Fifth Amendment,' she muttered, reluctant to expose herself for his triumph.

'Aha. . .in my book that's tantamount to a confession.' He ran his hands down her arms, causing the weirdest sensation in the pit of her stomach, and grasped hold of her hands. 'So now that we *both* know that I'm always right, I decree that you and I escape the glitz of decadent W4 for a few days and spend Christmas at my parents' house near Leominster. All in favour say "Aye".'

Five days and much trepidation later, Darcy's car, piled high with luggage, presents, one large cat-basket and Nathan, drove smoothly away from Bedford Park and headed for the M4 bun-fight around the Chiswick flyover and the route west.

Darcy seemed impervious to her nerves, and, as he concentrated on steering the Morgan through a traffic jam reminiscent of Aran knitting, Jem surreptitiously studied his face for signs of humanity.

It had all been so rapid, this transition from the relative safety of her new, comfortable life to the uncertainties that lay ahead. She did admit to herself that anything was better than confrontation with the dreaded 'Pitts', but Christmas with Darcy's relations ran that horror a close second. Even though she was apprehensive about the next few days, she couldn't have refused. And Darcy knows it, damn him! she thought.

She realised too that in many ways she had been getting far too complacent over these past weeks. She'd come to accept life in Darcy's house. Ceased to ask herself, 'What comes next? Where do I go from here?' Maybe, she conceded with a slight jolt, it was because she had been so very happy.

Happiness to Jem was not a positive emotion until it had been superseded by something else. Realising that deep happiness now just made the future all the less attractive.

After all, she mused, she had no real home. Nowhere to go if Darcy suddenly decided to throw her out. This feeling of being a displaced person—and just before Christmas, too, she realised indignantly—rammed it home to her just now precariously she was placed.

They spoke very little on the journey, Jem's nervousness making her abrupt to even the most casual of

Darcy's remarks. It was with mixed feelings that she eventually read the village name-plate of Eardisland and watched the picturesque black and white houses whiz by before they came to a halt beside a magnificent stone house.

'Here we are.' Darcy leaned back and sighed expansively. 'Welcome to the Manor.'

Two large retrievers and several small humans tumbled down the steps making a noisy welcome.

Darcy waded good-humouredly through this press-gang, steering a bemused Jem into the serenity of a warm oak-panelled hall.

'All right! Cease the clamour,' he shouted above the din. 'Here's the key. You lot unload the car, and perhaps—you never know—there might just be pirates' gold in the boot. But take care,' he called as the children raced away, 'of the wild beast in the back. It escaped from the zoo, and only the bravery of this young lady,' indicating Jem, 'saved us both from being eaten alive.'

Jem had barely a second to reflect on this new Darcy, the fond, roguish uncle, when a tall, grey-haired woman appeared, smiling broadly. As Darcy embraced her lovingly she caught sight of Jem and held out her hand welcomingly.

'Hello, I'm Margaret Lister. Darcy's mother. Do come into the sitting-room and get warm. I'll fetch you a cup of tea.' And she led Jem through a panelled door into a large, warmly lit room.

With a contented sigh Jem sank back into the crumpled chintz covering a fireside chair and gazed around her.

'The house is Jacobean,' Margaret Lister called as she moved off to make the tea. 'That's why you'll find that none of the furniture has more than three legs on the floor at any one time.' Jem stared round at the honey-gold walls and blond oak everywhere, and felt the mellowness seep through her. She felt privileged to share the age of this house with its owners.

Half-way through her second cup of tea the rest of the party returned, the noisy, intimate chatter from the hall making her feel slightly intrusive. A wave of loneliness threatened her serenity. She rose shyly as two women, Darcy's sisters by the look of them, and three large men, one of them so obviously Darcy's father as to draw a tentative smile to her lips, swept into the room.

'It's a better one than last year,' one of the sisters was saying. 'More like the Christmas trees we used to have as children.'

'Oh, yes, do you remember, Issa, that one that you and Darcy cajoled out of Grandpa that year? I think it had been rejected as being too big for Trafalgar Square!'

'Yes, and Darcy cut off the *top* to make it fit. . .silly chump. Oh, hello. . .' the woman called Issa said, spotting Jem. 'I beg your pardon. I had no idea we had visitors.'

'Hello,' Jem murmured. 'I'm a friend of Darcy's.'

'Oh, yes, of course. Ma said you were coming. Do you work at the college, too?'

'N-no. . .I'm just one of his students.'

'Oh, I see. Forgive me for being rude,' the second sister, introduced as Philippa, said curiously, 'but. . .I can't for the life of me place your accent. You're not American, are you?'

'No,' Jem smiled, knowing that her soft lilt mystified

most people. 'I'm what people wear funny hats about. I'm a Virgin Islander!'

'Really?' declared Philippa. 'You mean in the West Indies? How fascinating! Fancy giving up all that to live in rotten old London. You do live in London, I take it?'

'Yes, in Chiswick,' said Jem.

'Well, I never! So does Darcy. Do you live anywhere near him?'

And before she had had a chance to put a rein on her tongue she had blurted out, 'Oh, we live together!'

There was an infinitesimal pause during which Jem died three times, and then Clarissa said heartily, trying to overcome everyone's embarrassment, 'Well, yes. . .everyone does it nowadays, of course, but just a word of caution, dear. Ma is a bit old-fashioned, so do try to be discreet about it, won't you?'

With her mouth open ready to issue some useless denial to try to retrieve the situation, Jem was silenced by a voice from the doorway.

'You've no need to be concerned for Mother's delicate sensibilities, Issa. Yes, it's true. Jem and I do live in the same house, but then, so would any other normal married couple. Let me introduce you to Jemima Lister. My wife!'

CHAPTER SIX

THE congratulatory noises receded into a tunnel of fog as Jem fixed her shocked gaze on Darcy's face. Surely she must have misheard him? But the tense set of his jaw and the flinty look in his chill blue eyes told her she was not mistaken.

By her unguarded tongue she had made it necessary for him to reveal their marital status, though whose face he was saving—his, hers or his family's—she wasn't sure. That he was furious, she was!

She was angry with herself, too. With that one stupid remark she had wiped out all the warmth and pleasure she had begun so hopefully to envisage. The friendliness and humour of his family had completely won her over and she had thought that, with Darcy seemingly reaching out the hand of welcome, this year would cancel out all her previous lonely English Christmases.

But obviously not. The shutters had come down on Darcy's welcome.

She tried to brazen it out, imagining briefly that she could rise above the need for Darcy's approval, but she was surprised to find that conversation lost its edge and pleasure its savour without the curt nod or the brief, tight smile she had come to rely on as her stimulus. Living with him had seemed to be without incident, just an everyday story of domesticity, but it came as quite a shock to her to realise, as they all made their way to the sitting-room after dinner, that being in the shadow of his censure robbed her of cohesion. She felt adrift. Her thoughts lacked co-ordination. She felt as if she had come apart in the wash, and it was all the more alarming because it lay at the door of Darcy's disapproval.

Worse was to come.

'Darcy will show you to your room,' Mrs Lister said kindly as Jem stood at the foot of the massive Jacobean staircase. 'And welcome to the family, my dear. I'm so glad you decided to tell us after all.'

Jem felt a stab of guilt as she kissed her mother-in-law affectionately on the cheek and turned to follow Darcy, who was already half-way up the stairs. She felt churlish deceiving such a pleasant woman so flagrantly, but no such scruples seemed to be haunting the son of the house. It just seemed that he wished to get his unpleasant task over with as soon as possible as he marched on through the house, down some worn steps and through a low archway—he had to duck several times—until they eventually arrived at a small oak door. He lifted the wooden latch and stooped inside.

The room was lovely. A log fire crackled invitingly in the huge stone fireplace and a mirror on the wall reflected the gentle glow from two pink bedside lamps.

Jem trudged tiredly across the soft luxury of Chinese carpeting and sank down on the edge of the bed. Under normal circumstances she would have been thrilled to find herself sleeping in a genuine four-poster. Now she just wished that Darcy would leave so that she could curl up and hibernate away the gloom that was settling on the pit of her stomach like ballast.

But Darcy seemed to have no intention of leaving. He sat down by the fire and calmly began to unfasten his shoes. Then, after that, he pulled his azure sweater over his head and began to unbutton his shirt.

By this time Jem had sat bolt upright.

'What on earth are you doing?' she cried out in some alarm.

'Getting undressed for bed. What does it look as if I'm doing?'

'But you can't sleep here. This is my room. Isn't it?'

'This *is* your room. It's also *my* room. According to my mother married couples sleep together, so——'

The fearful implications of what he'd just said slowly percolated through her brain. 'I'm not sleeping with you!' she squeaked, leaping off the bed and rushing towards the door.

'Please yourself,' he remarked casually, removing his socks and unwinding himself slowly from the chair in order to begin unfastening his trousers. 'But, in that case, I haven't a clue where you *are* going to sleep. The house is chocka-block. No room at the inn, dear Jem, and the stables have standing room only!'

She turned from the door in a panic and was horrified to come face to face with her husband—absolutely stark naked. In her confusion and embarrassment she only had a second in which to register the beauty of the long, clean, muscular lines of his subtly tanned body before screwing up her eyes and pressing her hands across her face. It was mortifying to find that, when faced at last with the naked sight she had tried so hard to imagine during all her preparations for his sculpture, she degenerated into schoolgirl blushes.

'Oh. . .crumbs!' was all she could think of to say.

'Really?' he said drily, and then the bed-springs creaked and as the sheets rustled he called mockingly, 'Ready. . .coming or not! You can open your eyes now. I'm no longer offensive to a maiden's susceptibilities.'

Not wishing him to gloat over her fiery cheeks, she turned towards the mantelpiece before uncovering her face. What was she going to do? This was awful. It had never occurred to her downstairs that the natural conclusion of everybody would be that she and Darcy shared a bed. Married couples usually did. Why not this one? Well, there was only one thing for it, she decided. She would have to sit out the night in the chair by the fire. The one with Darcy's discarded clothing draped negligently across it.

She began moving his clothes.

'Now what are you up to?' he called in a blurred voice as if already half asleep. 'Come to bed. I'm not going to molest you.'

'You won't get the chance,' she said with feeling. 'I'm sleeping right here.'

'You'll freeze,' he muttered cosily. 'And serve you right. You were the one who got yourself into this hole, and if that's the way you choose to resolve it. . .all well and good.'

'Look, I'm sorry about blurting out that we live together. I know it sounded all wrong, but it is true after all!'

'Don't apologise!'

'But you seemed angry. I thought I'd upset you.'

'You did!'

'Oh. . .Well, you don't seem upset now.'

'I'm not. I've found that the situation has much to recommend it. . .But I will be in a minute if you don't shut up and come to bed.'

'I can't!' she wailed, twisting uncomfortably in the chair in order to peer at him round the tester. 'I can't sleep in the same bed as you.'

'It's legal!' he muttered into the pillow. 'Look,' after

a pause, 'I promise that all I want to do tonight is fall into a deep, luxurious sleep. My mind is on nothing else. *I* wanted this sitation as little as you obviously do, so you have nothing to fear. Aren't you being just a teeny bit presumptuous, anyway?' he added after a moment. 'After all, who has said I find you in the slightest bit attractive? Maybe, just maybe, Mrs Lister, I'm homosexual. . .Have you thought of that?'

No, she hadn't. A tremor ran up her back and she felt a sudden prick of tears behind her eyes. He couldn't be. Not Darcy. Not her husband.

'Are you?' she asked tremulously, although why it should interest her one way or the other, she wasn't sure.

'At this moment, my precious Jem, I am completely asexual. An amoeba. A blob. So do come to bed and cease this procrastination. Here. Will this help?'

And he placed a large bolster down the middle of the bed, gave it a beefy thump and turned over.

'There's the ref. Any foul play and he'll have me sent off. . .and that goes for you, too. Seduction gets a booking.'

He hadn't answered her question, but she knew it was the best she was going to get. With a sigh of resignation she tentatively lifted her long dark-blue skirt and then the white lace Victorian petticoat beneath it, and began to unhitch the bright red woolly stockings that helped to keep out the draught.

'Where's the bathroom?' she whispered, wondering if he really had fallen asleep or if the deep breathing was an act.

'The door next to the tallboy,' came the instant reply, and Jem smiled knowingly as she disappeared.

Twenty minutes later, bathed and with the washed

stockings dripping from the mantelpiece, she turned out the light and crept into the chair by the fading glow of the dying fire, wrapped herself in her coat and settled down to try to sleep.

It was amazing to her where the draughts came from. They whistled along the floor and paralysed her feet; one knifed through the seam in the chair and froze her kidneys, and a particularly vicious one found the space between her neck and the coat-collar, laying the foundation for future fibrositis. Darcy had been right. Within half an hour she was very cold indeed.

After another quarter she could stand it no longer. Shaking from head to toe, and wondering if this was the most foolish thing she had ever done in her life, she groped her way across the room and crept stiffly and gratefully under the covers.

There was no sign from the other side of the bolster. He was either asleep or lying doggo again, she thought, trying to curl up for warmth without causing any disturbance. But she was shaking so much, she could feel the massive headboard behind her juddering, and she knew that if she didn't stop she would be bound to wake him.

As if in confirmation he twitched convulsively and murmured something incomprehensible. She held her breath, and was just beginning to think she would never be able to relax again when, with a contented sigh, Darcy slid his naked arm across the no man's land of bolster and brought it to rest with his hand tantalisingly brushing her left breast.

A hot rush of surprise expanded through her blood, and as his fingers moved in a dream she felt the sweat of a sudden embryonic desire surge over her. It was shocking, frighteningly exciting. She felt the veils of mystery surrounding the sexuality of her body being softly blown aside. Disturbing needs began to awake in the deepest cavities of her senses.

Quickly she moved away, flustered by her own reaction to his sleeping touch. But already it was too late. Shaken, she rolled her head from side to side, vainly hoping that she could banish a vision from her mind, a vision all too real—of Darcy lying beside her, long, lean, beautiful. . .and naked.

As the word formed itself in her mind she gasped. What was she thinking? This had never happened to her before. Plenty of naked men had passed through her life at college—models, all studied and drawn with interest—but never had they ever visited her thoughts or disturbed the dormant chemistry of her body before. What had she done to conjure this genie of eroticism? Why, when Darcy scared her and angered her, ignored her, picked on her, should she all of a sudden find his touch the catalyst to her emotions?

She gave a trembling groan and began to turn away, but the faint noise must have disturbed him. With a muttered curse he propped himself up on to his elbow and groped across the bed, bumping his hand into her shoulder.

'What the hell have you got on?' he said thickly, through layers of sleep.

'A nightie,' she said neutrally, the constriction in her throat as he ran his fingers back and forth across the material nearly choking her.

'It feels like the loose cover for an armchair. I'll have to see this!'

The light blinded them both for a second, and Jem put her hand across her eyes to lessen the pain. When at last she spread her fingers wide enough to peep myopically through, she found Darcy grinning down at her.

'Whatever kind of garment do you call that? It could double as the storm jib on a barque!'

Feeling herself at a distinct disadvantage, Jem tried to be dignified. 'I made it myself. If you don't like it, just turn away and ignore it.'

'No. . .I love it,' he murmured consideringly. 'It's. . .it's. . .tantalising!' The corners of his smile began to droop as if a new seriousness dragged at his frivolity. Jem's heartbeat tripped as she watched his eyes darken. 'It's so chaste, one just has to know what goes on underneath. What it hides.' Their eyes held for a second. She read the dare, felt the power of his challenge as his hand slid up to her throat and slowly began an expert demolition on the many tiny buttons that penned her in.

'What am I going to find, Jem?' he whispered like the zephyr across a morning bay. 'What secrets am I about to uncover?'

Hypnotised by the softness of his voice she lay, mind and body paralysed. She knew she should resist, but the deft movement of his hand was getting lower, sapping her will, and she could feel the flutter of his breath condensing on her throat.

'You can't do this,' she whispered. 'You promised.'

'Yes, I did, didn't I?' he murmured in a lulling voice. 'Only I never imagined being placed in this intolerably intriguing position. Who could resist solving the conundrum of what goes on beneath this vestal night attire? Not me, I'm afraid. I'm not made of ice.'

As his voice sank to a whisper his eyes held hers transfixed. The pupils looked huge, overlapping the tempered steel of his irises and subjugating her with their voluptuousness.

'And I thought I was too tired to be tempted.' His voice was deep and husky. 'But if you must creep into my bed looking like Mary, Queen of Scots about to die, what do you expect?'

Jem could only let out a tiny gasp by way of protest as his cool hand slid between the open buttons, sending spasms of liquid gold jolting through her as his fingers trailed along her burning skin.

This was madness, she knew, lying immobile, allowing his hand to caress her throat, her shoulder, travel down across the pale freckles of her chest, down still further towards. . .

'No!' she cried hoarsely, wrenching her drugged mind back from the abyss of pleasure it had been about to plunge into. 'I mustn't let you.'

She sat up sharply, trying to brush him aside, to deny to herself how much his touch excited her, how very much she did want to let him.

She had never dreamed of this happening to her. The idea of being in bed with a man had barely ever entered her head, and then it had been only with slightly embarrassed amusement.

She *had* felt vague churning desires disturbing her nights occasionally after an illicit afternoon at the cinema wallowing in the charms of Jeremy Irons or Mel Gibson, but nothing serious. Nothing that swayed her from the one track she doggedly plodded. . .work.

And now here she was finding herself, not only in bed with a man. . .but with what a man!

Looking back on the weeks she had spent in his company, there had been nothing to indicate that she would be suffering this turmoil after only one brief glimpse of his nude body and the fleeting ecstasy of his touch. She had been obsessed by him, it was true, but only in so far as he affected her work. If he hadn't been present to be drawn, she had invariably dismissed him from her thoughts. Suddenly finding herself aglow and alive with this utterly new sensation, and all because of a person she was convinced she feared, was a very confusing state of affairs.

Now she knew why the kiss in his studio, all those weeks ago, had affected her so deeply. There was an element of treacherous chemistry working between them when their skin touched, and she didn't know how to handle it.

With a superhuman effort she turned away, dragging the bedclothes back in order to make her escape. But his hand grasped her wrist like an iron manacle.

'Why mustn't you?' he asked, his voice harsh and discordant.

'Because I would hate myself!' she cried, struggling to get free.

'Not because you don't want to, then? Not because the touch of my hand on your skin repulses you, or that ripe little body isn't crying out to give itself to me? No! It's because Miss Prim is squeamish.

'Well, let me tell you something, young woman,' he said as he tossed aside the useless bolster. 'It was never further from my thoughts to ravish you until you yourself made such a fuss about us being in the same bed. . .and whose fault was *that*? Whatever lustful thoughts I'm harbouring now are mostly your own doing.'

'Now you're trying to blame me! What have I done?' As she felt herself inexorably pulled towards him she realised how ineffectual her struggles were against his vastly superior strength. 'I never wanted this to happen.'

He looked down at her quizzically. 'No?' he murmured, raising one black brow. 'Are you sure there wasn't the tiniest grain of challenge in you to discover whether or not I was homosexual? Eh? That's a lure few women I know would be able to resist testing.'

She was stung by the possible truth of what he said, and counter-attacked sharply. 'And that's another thing,' she said, angry that the idea had only just struck her, 'I refuse to become just another one of the "women you know". I've heard them, wearing out the carpet by my bedroom door in Chiswick on their way up to your studio. I don't know what you get up to up there, and I don't care,' she added in what she hoped was a defiant tone, 'but I'm not going to join their ranks.'

He threw back his head and laughed, making his dishevelled silver hair fall across his forehead. 'Oh, Jemima Puddleduck, you're outrageous. . .But, no, you don't escape from me that easily,' he added as she tried to twist away from his grip while he seemed less vigilant.

With a lunge he grasped her by the shoulders and pinned her, struggling furiously, on to the bed. She began to panic, knowing how easily he could completely overpower her if he chose, and lashed out with her legs, thrashing and kicking. Her knee caught him sharply on the left thigh, and in an instant the teasing look vanished from his eyes and he held her down in deadly earnest, imprisoning her legs by the simple expedient of sliding on top of her.

Crushed, hardly able to breath, she lay there. She was furious with him, and with herself for allowing it to happen, but curiously she didn't feel afraid. She glared belligerently back at him, feeling a rush of excitement as she watched the expression on his face slowly change from baffled fury to one of sultry expectation.

As she licked her lips nervously she heard an anguished moan escape him, and then instantly her open mouth was crushed mercilessly under his. She tried to keep her eyes open, to retain some hold on sanity, but the room began to spin and, even though she tried to push him away, her muscles seemed to have turned to jelly and her bones to have melted away altogether.

Slowly he slackened his grip on her shoulders as he sensed the fight going out of her. She knew she should try, but the sweet fire that coursed through her as his tongue began to explore around her teeth, flickering and darting, was causing her resolve to disintegrate.

She found her thoughts becoming a confused jumble, and as she tentatively brought her tongue forwards so that it entwined with his, causing a reaction that startled her, she knew that the litigants of right and wrong in this case were going to have to go into court without her. She was opting out.

His hands joined in her subjugation. Swiftly the last of the buttons was ripped open and, with a skill that presupposed practice, he cast aside the voluminous nightdress and exposed the whole of Jem's perfectly rounded, creamy-white person for his eyes to feast on.

She knew that if she hadn't been so drugged with new and strange sensations the reality of lying naked in Darcy's arms would have caused her mind to miss a cog, but as it was she just revelled in the startling feel of her skin next to his, of the intimacy of his stomach and thighs pressing into hers, the sharp, sweet pain as his hand, at last, slid around her eager breast and began to torture her with a pleasure that never seemed to reach its peak, that always demanded more.

She moaned and arched her back, thrusting her pelvis provocatively upwards. Her hands moved like dainty crabs, nibbling delicately along his spine, down to the roundness of his tight, smooth bottom, scurrying daringly across and underneath to hide among the dark, mysterious caverns that her mind shied away from picturing.

But, novice though she was, she was learning fast. And her tutor was more than willing to teach. As his virtuoso hands brought forth a rapturous melody of excitement singing through her veins, all her instincts told her to reciprocate, to return to him all the pleasure, and more, that he was affording her.

Running her thumbs upwards, along his stomach and beneath the hollows of his arms, she sent sinuous tremors through him and he gasped, arching his neck, juddering convulsively against her. Blindly she leaned up, reaching out for him with her lips, running her moistened tongue down the curvature of his throat, squirming her body down the bed so that she could follow the line further. . .across his chest, sucking sweet, salty sovereigns of brown nipple, and then down, ever down, her mind and body fused into one featureless unit of passionate desire.

'Oh, you little witch!' he groaned, cupping her face in one hand and drawing her into a sitting position with the other.

They sat staring dazedly at one another, trying to take stock of the tornado that had just sucked them into its power.

'I want you,' Darcy murmured brokenly. 'I want to seduce that alabaster body.' As he spoke his hand described a feather-light parabola around her breast. 'But I mustn't. I have to control myself.'

The strings of desire that he had played so successfully, tuning them to an almost unendurable pitch, twanged and snapped at his words. The vibrations of unfulfilled needs took hold and she lost control. 'Why?' she cried brokenly, beginning to tremble. 'I don't mind. I. . .I want you, too.' She looked down at the space between them on the bed, unable to meet his eyes as the wrung-out confession hung in the air between them.

'I know you do. . .now. But that's only because it's all so new to you. Don't think I don't know what you're going through but, believe me, it will fade.'

He grabbed the duvet and wrapped it round her quivering shoulders. 'Don't look so dejected. Now that you know what you've been missing, you'll soon find a virile young stud to sweep you off your feet, I'm sure. And I promise I won't sue for adultery!'

As the pain melted from her eyes and splashed in salty misery on to the back of his hand he moved away. Taking a dressing-gown from the hook on the door, he put it on and turned to face her. 'There's a sofa in the dressing-room. I'll go in there and see if I can manage to tame my unruly instincts by tomorrow morning. I'm sorry things turned out the way they did.' And with a mock grave salute he exited.

The click of the latch rang like a knell through the silent room. Hardly able to believe what had happened, Jem sat, the words she could have used to try to make him stay beginning, too late, to form themselves in her mind.

But even as they crowded in, jostling her regret into

a deep and tender ache, she knew they would all have been useless. Suddenly he had had enough. Had it been conscience or distaste? What had she done? Why had he stopped in the middle of the most electrifying moment of her life? Surely he didn't think he was too old for her?

The questions raced around her head, filling her with the pain of uncertainty and the humiliation of rejection. He didn't want her.

What a fool she had made of herself. It must have been obvious that she was pushing herself, but she had been too blind to see, too lost in emotion. She fell forward on to the bed, burying her mortification in the pillow. Her skin prickled with embarrassment, and the deep gulf that opened in the pit of her stomach whenever she imagined his touch or the feel of his lips on her skin was double torture because she knew that, faced with the choice, she would do it all again.

The night dragged on, and she was plagued by the evocation of his presence. His clear blue eyes pierced her through the darkness, the moans of his pleasure rang through the silence and the thrill of his touch coursed through her loins, shattering her peace, banishing sleep to the devil.

The next morning he drove her into Hereford. With apparent disregard for any constaint she might be feeling, he totally overruled her feeble protests and insisted she accompany him.

Most of the journey was in silence, giving Jem plenty more opportunity to regret ever having set eyes on Darcy Lister, but the misery she felt when he was silent was compounded when he spoke.

'Last night wasn't supposed to happen, you know. I meant what I said when I married you—that I had no intention of seducing you. But I'm afraid the best laid schemes of mice and men. . .If it's any comfort to you, I spent a lousy night!'

'Oh,' she mumbled, not daring to turn his way. 'I'm sorry.'

'And so am I!' he laughed teasingly. 'I cursed myself for being so damned noble, but you're too naïve for the likes of me. Too sweet and gentle and. . .guileless. It would have been I who hated myself this morning if I'd given in to my baser nature. Not you!'

She found it terribly difficult to tidy her emotions into recognisable compartments. Anger muddled in with regret, and relief that he was speaking about it, almost crowded embarrassment right out altogether. A strange amalgam won the day.

'I'm not a child,' she said, clearly and defiantly. 'I'm old enough to make up my own mind. And last night. . .I wanted you to make love to me.' There. . .she'd said it! Her palms were wet and her heart was thumping triple time, but, as far as she was concerned, she had cleared the air.

'I know. It was very important to you, I could tell. But it's a huge step to take, you know. It's not something to be thrown away on the first man who has the temerity to ask.'

'You didn't ask. . .you nearly just took. But I wouldn't have minded. Honestly.'

'You're a funny child,' he said reflectively. 'So unworldly and yet so forthright. I find your candour rather uncomfortable at times. It reminds me of when I was your age. I used to have that in-built conviction once that people were basically decent—noble even! That everything would come out right if only a few simple changes were made. I learned by experience. I got older and more cynical, but I do have a few mild regrets when I look at your innocence now. Everything's black and white to you, isn't it? No grey shades of doubt or disillusion?'

She looked at him quizzically. 'What are *you* disillusioned about?' she asked. 'Your lack of innocence, or the fact that I'll soon lose mine?'

'How soon?' He seemed to be having difficulty with his voice.

'Oh, I don't just mean the physical kind,' Jem hastened to correct the conclusion he'd jumped to, 'but it's not such a disaster to lose some of it. If you're positive and hopeful and look on life as a pleasurable challenge, well, then, the loss of a bit of inexperience is an asset. Surely?'

'That's a Pollyanna philosophy I find it difficult to live with, Jem. The world is a big, ugly place full of self-seekers and sharks, and the naïve grow up all too quickly. You're certainly right that losing innocence can be an advantage. I'm just sad that it has to be so brutal.'

'It doesn't *have* to be. It all depends on the teacher, doesn't it?'

He grunted and gave her an odd look as he swung the car into a waiting gap.

'Right, Miss *Ingénue*,' he muttered, 'your teacher awaits. For starters, the ethnic Mongolian look,' he plucked at the cloak she was wearing, 'is about to be dashed on to the scrap-heap of experience!' And he dragged her, protesting, into a singularly exclusive-looking boutique.

Staggering beneath the weight of bags and boxes, they relayed back and forth to the car. Clothes, sumptuous and vivid, at prices Jem hardly dared contemplate, were tossed irreverently around the back seat.

Leather boots and shoes, jewellery, make-up—all followed with equal negligence until the small rear window was virtually obscured by flashy carriers and tissue paper.

Jem was stunned. Never in all her life had she seen so much money exchange hands, and to realise that she was the beneficiary made her feel, to her confusion, somewhat resentful. It was all very well for this rich man to flash his wealth under her nose, but she felt that it was an imposition to thrust these gorgeous clothes at her and expect her to accept them gratefully just to appease some weird sense of philanthropy on his part.

She knew she should refuse to accept them, and she did try, but he dismissed her protests.

'You don't like the silk suit?'

'Yes. . .it's beautiful. It's just that——'

'You don't think it suits *you*?'

'Oh, no. It's not that. . .I——'

'I was going to say. . .because, personally, I've never seen a garment come so alive or make the person inside it so glamorously—um. . .' he studied her contemplatively for a second '. . .alluring!'

Jem blushed hotly, but persevered. 'I just can't accept it. Or any of them,' she added defiantly.

'Why ever not?' He found his credit card again. 'It's a Christmas present.'

'But everything's so expensive.' She felt anger building to an explosion inside her.

'I can afford it.'

'Oh, you pig-headed, arrogant, selfish swine!' she burst out, to the disapproval of an unctuous sales lady. 'I don't care if you have all the money in the world. I don't want your charity. There! That's plain enough, isn't it?'

He cast a strange, disturbing glance her way. For one split second she could have sworn pangs of hurt pierced her from his eyes, but the next moment the harshness of his voice dispelled the illusion.

'Oh, very, Jemima dear! So let me make *myself* plain, too. I am a tolerant man, but I will not have my wife slopping around my parents' house at Christmastime looking like a tatterdemalion. I'm buying you these clothes in order to dispel the impression, which you seem to revel in, that you *enjoy* jumble-sale rejects.'

Only the sightseers, discreetly snooping, stopped her from hitting him. A lurch of pain caught her in the stomach.

'I can wear what I like.'

'Do you *like* those?' He indicated the church-bazaar skirt, too big round the waist, and a velvet shirt whose pile had worn away in prominent spots. The scorn in his voice had shrivelled her self-confidence.

'The colours are lovely, yes. . .and,' she tried to appear defiant, 'I like the style.'

'But the cut and the finish are rubbish. They were rubbish when they were new. Now they're just shabby rubbish.'

'You make me sound like a down-and-out,' she whispered resentfully, beginning to haul herself out of the multi-coloured jacket he was trying to buy. 'But I'd rather be that, and have some self-respect left, than be a popinjay product of your toffee-nosed pride. You can take everything back. I'm not wearing a single item.'

He hadn't threatened or cajoled.

'Pity!' he'd said offhandedly. 'You looked so stunning, too. Never mind. Perhaps circumstances will persuade you otherwise.'

What those circumstances could be she had had ample time to cogitate on as they drove silently home.

It seemed that from armed neutrality in London they had broken into full hostilities in the tension-charged closeness forced upon them at the Manor. Jem felt that she regretted the passing of their peace, but she had to admit to a sneaking sense of exhilaration as they warred. Her cheeks glowed, her skin felt softer and more alive, and she knew her eyes were bright from the lamplit reflections she glimpsed occasionally in the window of the car. He might be hateful, but she couldn't deny the impact he was having on her psyche.

She was just beginning to try out a rueful grin at the sight they must have presented in the dress shop, hissing malevolence at each other as the general public enjoyed a ringside seat, when Darcy drew the car to a halt outside the house.

'Look who's here.' He spoke for the first time since leaving Hereford, and his voice overpowered the confined cockpit inside the small car.

She couldn't define what emotion was uppermost in his tone. Mockery? Pleasure? Boredom? But she knew her own the instant she caught sight of the tall, elegant silhouette in the light from the front door. Dread and disappointment, closely followed by crushing inadequacy.

She gasped in shock, swivelling to face Darcy. 'You toad!' she muttered. 'You scheming liar. You said she was house-sitting in London. You *knew* she was coming here, didn't you?'

He didn't reply as, starkly glamorous in black and

white crêpe, Venetia Pitt swayed down the steps towards them, ostentatiously keeping out the cold with the help of a blue fox stole.

'Well, I'm not going to hang around to be used as cannon-fodder.' She sank her voice to a low purr. 'I think you're pretty despicable, Darcy, to have set this up.'

She tried to escape from the car as the protective expanse of gravel separating them from Venetia dwindled before her eyes, but Darcy's hand leapt out in the gloom and held on to her arm. 'After such rude and uncivilised comments, Miss Hell Cat, I'd be quite justified in putting you across my knee!' Jem struggled in righteous indignation, but he kept his grip firm. 'However, we only have two seconds before she's at the car. . .so listen.

'I did not lie to you, and I didn't scheme, either. Venetia rang my mother yesterday, and it turns out I'd left some presents behind, so Ma invited her to bring them down and spend Christmas with us. Which she has duly done.'

'You must have left the presents on purpose,' Jem mumbled ungraciously, horrified that the calm atmosphere of this family Christmas was being so rudely shattered.

Darcy pointedly ignored her. 'And the clothes I bought you today were partly compensation. You could at least be *dressed* as expensively as her——'

'Even if I don't look nearly as good. Isn't that what you were going to say?' She glared at him, hotly angry.

'No!' He sighed wearily. 'I wasn't going to say that at all. I just, in my misguidedly non-female approach to the situation, imagined that you'd prefer to meet Ms

Pitt on equal terms instead of being thrown to her like a chicken at a Black Mass. I see I was wrong.'

With a start Jem realised that Venetia was only a couple of yards from the bonnet of the car, a smile on her lips, but a gleam in her eye. She thought of the worn, baggy clothes she'd put out for Christmas Day, the scuffed and down-at-heel shoes, and she looked again at the *svelte* distinction of Venetia's cleverly cut dress and expensive boots.

She saw Darcy about to put out his hand to open the car door and, giving herself no time to feel embarrassed by her lightning about-face, 'Darcy,' she whispered urgently, 'have I left apologies too late? I think maybe you were right, and these "circumstances" have persuaded me to change my mind. Can I just *borrow* the clothes for Christmas? Please?'

Venetia was startled, seconds later, to find the tranquillity of the night shattered by twin shouts of explosive laughter.

CHAPTER SEVEN

JEM didn't laugh for long.

Venetia's fell influence pervaded the house, and time seemed heavier with her presence. She lost no opportunity to discomfit Jem if she could, snaking herself round Darcy with blatant eroticism, or instigating disparaging discussions on the parlous state of the art school system and its output. Naming no names, but watch my eyes.

Jem was rather shocked that Darcy didn't tell Venetia that they were married in order to stem this embarrassing behaviour, but when she tentatively remarked on it he just said coldly, 'I've told my family to keep it under their hats because I don't want to upset her over Christmas. Surely you can see that?'

Jem supposed, reluctantly, that she did see.

But she did find a power over Venetia which was richly stimulating. The power of her new clothes. Her miraculous transformation from ragamuffin to chic sophisticate obviously rocked Venetia's perspective to its foundation.

She made some pointed remarks about girls with muddy complexions being so lucky to be able to wear garish colours, but ended up looking pettish beside the compliments of the rest of the company.

Darcy said nothing, and Jem puzzled over the motive behind his treating her so lavishly. It couldn't just be altruism, she felt sure, nor, she reasoned despondently as she lay tucked up in her solitary bed, was it from any wish to buy her body, because earlier he had held a brief, whispered conversation with someone by the bedroom door and then gone away. Jem found herself coming to an inevitable conclusion and spent the aeons till his return to the dressing-room unwillingly imagining some tumbling bedroom assignation with Venetia.

She was crestfallen to realise now just why he'd been so 'noble' the night before. Not for her sake, that was for sure, but because he knew who would be arriving the following day.

The high-pitched clamour of excited children broke through Jem's protective oblivion the next morning. Christmas Day had arrived!

Blearily, she stumbled along the dark corridor where 'Oohs' and 'aahs' drew her towards a lighted doorway. Inside there was a hotch potch assortment of boys and girls, all delving and ripping and shrieking with delight.

'Oh, Auntie Jem!' one little girl called, catching sight of her. 'Thank you, thank you!' She rushed forwards, hugging Jem unselfconsciously. Jem was baffled. She'd only bought some sweets to be shared among them, not having known of their existence two days ago.

'I don't think it's me you should be thanking, love,' she began cautiously. 'Let's have a look at the label, shall we?'

But as she began to examine the tattered wrapping a slow flush crept over her. 'To Sophie,' it read, 'Love from Uncle Darcy and Auntie Jem.' And clutched to the small bosom of Sophie, who was beaming up at her, was an exquisite baby doll dressed to the nines in the latest fashion in layette.

'Yes, darling, you're right. How foolish of me,' Jem mumbled. 'What have you decided to call her?' And as the child prattled on about the doll, Jem sank to the floor amid the debris and began surreptitiously spying out more labels in Darcy's bold writing with her name appended. There were a lot.

It was a pleasant feeling sitting among these children, accepted and acknowledged as another member of their family. She didn't try to force the pace with them, and was rewarded by a frankness and lack of affectation that charmed her.

'Move over, Auntie!' said a deep voice in her ear. 'We childless couples need room on the floor to enjoy the action.' Darcy, in pyjamas and dressing-gown, squatted by her side, handing her a mug of tea and a biscuit. He seemed totally oblivious to the atmosphere of cutting disapproval that Jem was endeavouring to freeze him out with, and he began blithely, 'This is one of the most magical times in life. I love watching the expressions on their faces; wonderment and avarice in equal parts.'

When she didn't reply his lip quirked, 'And there's no polite pretence. If you don't like something it's "Yuk" and let the world know.'

Jem tried to ignore him, but he continued remorselessly. 'We could learn something from that, eh, Jemima? More honesty, more straightforward simplicity between us? How do you feel about that?'

She wasn't sure how she felt about it. What did he mean? That he should tell her she was in the way of his plans and she should tactfully remove herself? That she should tell him how much she disliked him? That the whole marriage *à la mode* had been a disaster and that they should both agree to a speedy separation? What else could he be implying?

With an oddly flat resignation, she nodded. 'Well,

yes, if that's how you want it, but I thought I had been fairly honest with you.'

He was looking at her, an expression of intense concentration on his face, as if he was memorising every feature. 'You have, and I've told you it can be pretty disturbing at times, but there is an honesty *I've* been holding back on which I feel I ought to come clean about.'

He never got the chance.

The clop of hard-soled mules on the polished oak floor sounded a split second before a tired, petulant voice said, 'So this is where the row's coming from. You do know it's only half-past six? Some people are trying to sleep!'

If she didn't look so disagreeable, Jem thought, Venetia would be at her most attractive at this ungodly hour. Her pale hair billowed loosely round her small, heart-shaped face, and the lack of her usual gaudy make-up revealed pretty features. Jem couldn't help a feeling of dismay. So this was what Darcy found so attractive! No wonder he'd stayed away so long last night.

Venetia clomped drowsily into the room, surveying the devastation with distaste, and from then on dominated the proceedings.

'Robert, open that one next before it gets trodden on. Sophie, don't just throw your paper on the floor. Put it in the basket. . .Oh, how *super*, Kate. Can I have a go? I always wanted one of those.'

The children shifted uneasily. Jem, after enduring all she could stomach of Venetia's gushing, quietly left the room, wondering at the blindness of his love.

The tree, dominating the hall, was the congregation point after church and a late breakfast. With a pale gold sherry that matched her new cords, Jem settled down on the periphery to watch the fun of present-giving.

Her offerings, hastily bought the day before, were accepted with gratifying pleasure, and she was delighted with the expensively packaged toiletries that Darcy's family had been thoughtful enough to give her.

Venetia gave Darcy a cut-glass decanter, and Darcy gave Venetia lead-crystal wine-glasses. A case of great minds, thought Jem, trying not to feel too savage during this season of goodwill.

As the last childish face dissolved into rapture, and everyone was preparing to go about their separate occasions till lunchtime, Darcy suddenly called out from deep in the tree, 'Hang on, everyone. There's one more.'

'Oh, who's it for, Uncle Darcy?' piped Sophie eagerly, ever hopeful.

Darcy held the package under the lights, pretending to have difficulty reading the name. It just says "Jem" he muttered as Sophie snatched the flat box from him and weaved her way to Jem's side.

'Open it. Open it!' she urged as Jem, feelings of inexplicable trepidation seizing her, fumbled with the glossy wrapping.

Many times afterwards she relived that moment.

Darcy had watched her intently, a secretive, mocking look in his eyes, and as she had drawn the flimsy satin nightdress from its wrapping and tentatively held its pale coral length against herself he had smiled insolently.

The sight of his face now, as she lay in bed dodging well-meaning head butts from Ali, kept thrusting itself into her imagination: arrogance vying with self-conceit.

A fierce combination of hostility and physical desire surged through her every time she thought of the obvious reasoning behind his gift. Damn him! His message was clear. 'Wear this and it'll really arouse my baser instincts.' And, Jem realised with self-disgust, her own, too. Her anger rose. How had he the gall to treat her, his wife, like this, with his mistress happily established somewhere else in the house and more than willing to accommodate his needs? And it made her crosser still to know that she had no real grounds for complaint. She knew as well as he that she was not his real wife, and had never been intended to be. Being self-righteous wasn't going to change anything.

'So there you are, Jemima,' Venetia's voice rang out as Jem emerged at the head of the stairs the next morning. 'You're the last one to be accounted for. Where have you been?'

Jem turned to Clarissa. 'I'm sorry. Am I late?'

'Oh, no, it's not that——' Clarissa began, seemingly uncomfortable at Venetia's bossiness.

'No, my dear. Poor Venetia is concerned that you should know about the slight hiccup there's been in the smoothly run Lister household.' The furrows across her brow belied Margaret Lister's light words.

'You know my little. . .what I call my Degas. . .sculpture of the ballet dancer?'

'Oh, yes. I was admiring it last night. It's so incredibly like his work, isn't it?'

'Yes. We're not sure if maybe it isn't a *real* Degas, but we've never dared to have it valued just in case the insurers tell us to put it out of harm's way in a bank vault, or something. I suppose they'd be right, considering that I found it this morning—broken.'

'Broken? Oh, no!'

'Oh, yes!' Venetia's softly insidious voice crept over Jem's shoulder. 'You didn't notice anything wrong, did you, last night? When you were looking at it before you went to bed?'

'No,' Jem said, a trifle defensively, knowing how much Venetia would love her to be in the wrong. 'No, I left it on its plinth in the study. I didn't touch it. . .honestly.'

'Oh, I wouldn't dream of suggesting that you'd do it deliberately,' Venetia murmured with oily sincerity, 'but I did wonder. . .' she allowed the suspense to build as she paused fractionally to pluck imaginary hairs off the sleeve of her jersey-silk tube-dress '. . .whether perhaps you forgot to close the door. Maybe your cat. . .what's his name? Harry? You know how curious cats are.' She turned deferentially to Mrs Lister. 'That's one of the reasons you don't have a cat, isn't it, Margaret? They seem to get everywhere.'

Margaret Lister was about to reply, but Venetia bore inexorably on.

'And he could so *easily* have got into the study, and——'

Jem decided it was time to intervene. 'But he was with me. He was upstairs in my bedroom all night. Ask. . .' Darcy, she nearly said, and felt the sharp pain as she bit her tongue just in time.

Darcy had seen him curled up in the chair by the fire. 'The eunuch guarding the virgin bride!' he had called mockingly as he passed through to the dressing-room. Darcy had definitely seen him. But she knew how impossible it would be to confess that to Venetia.

And then it occurred to her. Where was Darcy? While she was enduring trial by insinuation, where was the chief witness? She watched the carefully neutral faces of her recently acknowledged in-laws and felt a pang of need for his urbanity. For his slicing common sense that aways reduced excitability and exaggeration to its inevitable silliness.

'. . .ask. . .ask him.' She finished her sentence lamely, bringing a derisive smile to Venetia's face.

'I would if he could talk,' she said, playing to her audience, 'but isn't that odd? I could have *sworn* I saw him in the hall last night. About half-past eleven. Just after you'd gone to bed. Are you sure he was with you?'

'Positive,' said Jem, feeling the trap squeezing shut.

Venetia smiled like an asp. 'Funny. . .well. . .I must have been mistaken. But I don't usually see things that aren't there. Perhaps I need glasses like you, Jemima.' Her laughter tinkled prettily round the drawing-room.

Jem felt the impossibility of trying to counter the wide-eyed sincerity that Venetia exuded. With every denial Venetia became more convincing, more earnestly seeking after the truth. Jem felt defeat staring her in the face and the conviction growing among the company that she, through her cat, was responsible for the 'Degas' accident.

Speculation seemed superfluous a few moments later.

'Mummy. . .Mummy. . .Look who I've found.' Ten-year-old Angus stood in the doorway, Ali dangling like a moth-eaten Golden Fleece from his right arm. 'He was in the study, nosing about round the Degas plinth.'

Venetia's expression said it all. She managed to combine smugness with sanctimony while also giving off an air of sorrowful disillusionment. It was a masterly performance.

In that instant Jem knew how comprehensively she

had been set up. No amount of denial was going to clear her properly of suspicion. Darcy's mother and sisters had smiled at her in a dreamy sort of way when she'd said, with perhaps a hint too much vehemence, 'He was upstairs in my bedroom all night.' But she knew she would be tainted now as someone who shirked her responsibilities, who'd deny a glaring truth. It made her feel sick at heart.

'What're all the long faces about? Have I interrupted a tolling of the Lutine Bell?'

'Darcy!' Jem called breathlessly amid the hubub of voices that heralded his arrival. 'You've got to tell them.'

'Tell them what?' he asked quizzically.

'That Ali didn't break your mother's Degas.'

'It's only the little finger, Darcy. Nothing to worry about unduly.'

But Darcy ignored his mother. 'Why?' he asked, piercing Jem with a hard stare.

'Because he didn't!' she cried desperately. 'Venetia says she saw him in the hall at half-past eleven, but he was asleep in that chair in my bedroom all night, so she can't have done.'

Darcy took a swift look around the room, taking in the charged atmosphere. With a sudden, abrupt gesture he scooped the cat out of Angus's arms. 'Ali, me old fruit, you didn't go breaking ballerina's fingers, did you?' He looked up contritely. 'I'm sorry, Mother. I shall have to take the blame. It was all my fault. Do you forgive me?'

Relief flooded round the room as everyone began to talk and make amends to Ali, and it was only Jem who noticed a brief flash of bafflement that Venetia cast in

Darcy's direction before she, too, began bridge-building.

'You must have a ghost, Margaret,' she teased as Clarissa pondered on what could have been creeping through the hall so late at night. 'I've often thought I must be psychic, and this is the perfect place to find out!'

The matter was dismissed and the day continued, but Jem felt the injustice festering through everything she tried to do.

'She did it on purpose,' she hissed breathlessly, trying to keep pace with Darcy as they both hurried to change for dinner that evening. 'She tried to make them think that Ali had broken that statue.' It was the unfairness of it that stuck in her throat.

'Whatever makes you think that Venetia would do a thing like that?' he murmured smoothly, seeming not to care that he sounded totally unconvincing.

'Because she hates me and wants to hurt me, why else? And don't stand there mocking me!' she shouted, slamming their bedroom door as she followed him in. 'It may all be hysterically funny to you, but it's horrible for me.'

'Now, now, don't get so worked up. It's only——'

'Stop patronising me!' she stormed. 'Ever since that woman arrived you've treated me like an imbecile. The final insult was that whorish nightdress. I suppose you get a cheap thrill imagining me in it? Well——'

'No, Jem, there you're wrong. From the amount of money that thing cost, it gives me a very expensive thrill. But a thrill, nevertheless.'

'You lecher!' she spat. 'Well, I've had enough. I want to go home. I. . .'

She felt his eyes widen and, to hide the sudden

confusion that overwhelmed her at her own slip of the tongue, she took refuge in sarcasm.

'Home! Ha, that's a laugh, isn't it? Where is my home? I haven't got one.'

'You know my house is your house,' Darcy said with a strange, quiet urgency, grasping hold of her shoulders in a fierce grip.

She was startled by his touch, and the sensual reaction it caused made her accentuate her hostility.

'Oh, yes. . .as long as I'm a good little wife and do as I'm told I'm allowed to live under your roof. What happens when I don't toe the line, though? When I don't treat Darcy Lister as if the sun shone out of his backside? What happens then? I'm out on my ear!'

'Calm down, will you? I'm not going to throw you out.' His hands tightened as he gave her an admonishing shake.

She knew she was getting hysterical, but the ordeal she had suffered had unnerved her. She felt denigrated, debased. The humiliation of the insinuation still stung painfully. The fact that her pulse quickened alarmingly when his hands gripped her only made her feel more sickened with him. . .and herself. Unaware of the strangely vulnerable expression on her face, Jem brought her gaze up to do battle with Darcy's as she struggled mightily to free herself from his clasp.

'Let go of me, you great hulk,' she gasped, pushing at his chest.

'What? After you've just been so abominably rude to me? I think I'd be more than justified in tanning your hide.'

'You wouldn't!' she breathed, eyes like the third tinder-box dog. 'It would be assault.'

'Not if you enjoyed it.' He chuckled as a gasp of

outrage escaped her, and without thinking she hit him, hard, across the face. A spasm of fear leapt through her as she realised what a foolhardy thing she had just done.

His eyes began to narrow and the long, dark lashes that swept down camouflaged his lurking expression. 'You little devil,' was all he said before she found her senses pulverised by the sudden onslaught of his lips crushing hers. It was totally unexpected, and for one wild moment she felt a cataclysm of urgent desire overwhelm her. The need she felt for him sent turbulent seas of heat washing over her, and she clung to him, pressing herself as close as his hard muscles would allow. Returning his kiss. Catching his lips, his tongue between her teeth, biting until she was sure she tasted blood.

And, as suddenly, it was over. Icy reason sliced through the turmoil in her brain. He was using her. He was manipulating her body to gain control of her mind. With a force that took him by surprise she wrenched herself out of his arms. That the expression she read on his face was not the unprincipled triumph she had expected didn't sink in with Jem. She interpreted what she wanted to interpret. Calculated lust was what she saw, and it helped her to come to some kind of terms with the shame prickling through her at the memory of her own frenzied abandon. Making him the scapegoat would, in part, ease some of her own guilt.

'How dare you?' she cried, backing away on legs that threatened to collapse under her. 'You disgust me with your games. I'm not going to become just one more notch on your sexual tallystick. I warn you,' she squeaked, as his eyes narrowed and he took a pace towards her, 'if you come any closer, I'll scream.'

With an air of weary resignation he shrugged. 'Have it your own way. I seem to have been battering my head against a brick wall with you, don't I? Whichever stand I take, good or bad, I can't win. "Life", Mrs Lister. Living. You seem to have no conception of the word.'

'No. Not if it involves living it to your dictation. I've had enough of being used as an experiment in titillation. I'm——'

'Well, have no fear,' he interrupted contemptuously. 'You won't be faced with it any more.' He gathered up a few scattered garments and strode to the door. 'Tonight I sleep in more pleasant surroundings, so. . .you can lie safely in your barren bed and I hope it brings you joy!'

Tears of anger started in her eyes as the door clicked shut behind him. He was insufferable. He had used her. She felt sure he had set her up just now in order to have a weapon to use against her. So that he could walk out and to Venetia's bed and make it look as though she'd sent him there. 'Of all the double-dealing hypocrites!' she exploded, sobbing as if her heart would break. The fact that she couldn't now bear to send her mind probing into the imagined intimacies of her husband and the Scarlet Woman made it all the more distressing.

With a fatalism that began almost at once to calm her, she knew that she had to leave. To stay, the cat's paw in Darcy's machinations and the victim of Venetia's satanic plots, would be far too akin to oriental torture.

The most difficult part of walking out was trying to explain, in a long and involved note to Mrs Lister, just why it had become necessary for her to go, but later on that night, cat-basket in one hand and just the clothes she'd arrived with in a battered holdall in the other, she had trudged gloomily along the road into Leominster to catch the early morning bus back to London.

The echoes of the warmth of Darcy's family helped to sustain her through the stop-start journey by country bus, but later the coldness of Darcy's eye and Venetia's pallid smirk bore her dubious company from the outskirts of Swindon until she limped, Ali mysteriously having grown to ten and a half stones, down the steps of Yvonne's basement flat in Ealing. The landlady was not over-enthusiastic about letting her into the empty flat, but her frail, transparent appearance and the sad exhaustion in her eyes eventually won her the spare key.

On their return several days later, and after some elaborate bending of the truth by Jem, Yvonne and Mike let her cadge a mattress on the living-room floor until she could find herself a room.

She became aware of how odd it felt not to be woken every morning by the chink of cup and saucer on the bedside table, not to hear off-key singing from the bathroom that always compelled her lips to twitch in a silly grin, not to feel a start of anticipation when the key scraped in the latch. 'It's like losing a sick headache,' she told herself irritably. 'You wonder what's missing.'

But that theory didn't quite hold water when she walked into college on the first day of the spring term. Losing sick headaches didn't make you go weak at the knees.

'Jemima!' He seemed to have been hiding behind the main door, waiting in ambush. 'Where the hell have you been?'

Her hackles rose instantly, cancelling out the sudden

quickening of her heartbeat. 'Keeping out of your way. Where do you think?'

Instead of answering, he grasped her by the wrist and propelled her into the empty staffroom.

'You've led me a caper. I've searched this damned city from toe-hole to eye-socket trying to find you,' he muttered sternly. 'What were you playing at, hiding from me like that?'

'You couldn't care less if I fell down a hole in the road,' she began, bitterly contemptuous of his pride that wouldn't let her go without his permission. 'I should imagine that you and Ms Pitt had a more enjoyable time without me.'

He ignored her blustering defiance, looking steadily at her with an expression of exasperation mingled with what looked suspiciously like compassion. 'So young,' he murmured contemplatively. 'I'm afraid, my childlike Jem, you're going to grow up with a bump. I've got a message for you.'

His manner became grave and he led her towards a cluttered chair, sweeping papers and someone's old cardigan on to the floor abstractedly. 'Sit down.'

At last Jem began to realise that it was not truculence that made him appear so forceful and aggressive, but some other emotion—one he seemed to find difficulty in expressing. Her heart began to pound as uncertainty overcame her.

'Does the name Mrs Stewart mean anything to you?'

Jem groped in her memory before nodding. 'She runs the hotel where Grandma works. . .Why?'

'She phoned from Tortola three days ago asking for you. I'm afraid your grandmother is gravely ill.'

It took a second or two to impinge before the shock

spread through her like intravenous ice. 'Grandma?' she whispered. 'Oh, no. What's the matter with her?'

'She fell and broke her hip four weeks ago. She didn't want anyone to tell you, apparently, in case it spoiled your Christmas.'

'Oh, Grandma. Poor, sweet, foolish Grandma.' She felt slight impatience at her grandmother's self-sacrifice. 'But hips mend, don't they? Surely she's getting. . .?'

'Yes, hips do mend, but she contracted pneumonia while she was in hospital and, according to Mrs Stewart, is getting gradually worse.'

'Oh, no! Oh, no, no. . .no!' The full horror of what could happen suddenly hit her. Her grandmother, the only person in the world who loved her, who cared two hoots what became of her, could leave her alone and friendless. Could die.

'She won't die, though. I shan't let her. I shall go to Tortola and care for her and make her better, that's what I'll do. I'll go today. I'll. . .I'll. . .' Her stormy pacing gradually ceased as she realised the impossibility of what she was saying, 'How can I go? I've no money. Nothing to sell. . .' A new madness seized her. 'I'll go to the bank and offer my sculptures as security. . .I'll. . .' She already knew how flailingly useless she sounded, how lost her cause. 'Oh, what am I going to do?'

Obviously forgotten, Darcy watched as she clutched at and then discarded schemes and nightmares. 'Jem,' he called softly, but she didn't hear him. 'Jem, listen.'

She turned a blank mask towards him, not seeing him, only hearing his voice down a hollow tube. The anguish behind her glazed eyes made him suddenly catch his breath, and before she realised what was happening he was cradling her to his chest as if it was the most natural thing in the world.

'Don't worry, my little jewel, don't worry. She'll be all right,' he whispered, his breath flutteriing her hair as she leant, like a small totem-pole, against him.

She felt the helpless urgency of a broken bird, needing to escape yet grounded by fate. The walls of panic began to close over her. 'But I've got to *see* her. I can't leave her to suffer, all those miles away, and not go to her.'

'You shall. I've got your ticket here, all ready. That's why I've been searching for you so frantically.'

She heard the deep growl of his voice through the ear that was pressed to his chest. She must have misheard.

'You've got a ticket for me?'

'An open-ended return so that you can stay just as long as it takes.'

'Oh, Darcy, I'm sorry.' Suddenly she felt very tired. It was such a relief to relinquish the responsibility of her immediate life on to the strong, capable shoulders of the man on whom she found herself leaning in more ways than one. 'I'm sorry I was so nasty. I thought. . .you sounded angry, so I. . .was angry back.'

He patted her shoulder in an avuncular way. 'Little cat,' he muttered, abruptly clearing his throat as the words became tangled in his vocal chords. 'I'll forgive you this time. But come on,' he stood away from her, shaking himself into brisk purposefulness, 'or you'll never catch that plane this evening. You do have a passport, I take it?'

Later that night, Jem blindly returned the plastic smile of the girl checking her ticket for Flight 509 to

Antigua. Darcy had thought of everything, even down to hand-made chocolates, a gift for her gran. She turned to smile her thanks, only to catch a momentary glimpse of his back as he disappeared into the crowd. He had slipped away.

On a whim she kissed the tips of her fingers and blew a silent thank-you across the airport lounge. What would she have done without him?

With optimistic fervour she turned and headed towards Passport Control.

CHAPTER EIGHT

THE tropical sun was piercing holes in the threadbare curtain as Jem awoke to the familiar chink of cup and saucer.

'Thank you,' she murmured in a dazed kind of voice, holding out her hand to take the tea, 'but you shouldn't have. . .really. . .It's very rude of the hostess to allow the guest to bring her tea in bed.'

'Habit!' Darcy said, eyeing her speculatively. 'And, in any case, I like my morning tea in the morning. I think I'd have got rather thirsty by now!' He grinned slowly, blunting the edges of his barbed comment.

'I can't see my watch. What time is it?' She screwed up her eyes in an effort to read the battered art deco clock sullenly ticking on a massive chest of drawers at the far end of the long, low room.

'My watch is still on London time,' he said, 'and that clock's slow.' He stepped briskly across the room to open the curtains. 'But it's past one.'

'One in the afternoon? Never!' she gasped, just stopping herself from leaping out of bed in the flimsy cotton nightie she was wearing. 'Oh, why didn't you wake me before?'

'Because you needed the sleep. I hardly recognised you when I arrived last night. You looked. . .' He turned to face her, the glare from the window hiding his expression in haloed darkness. 'You looked. . .empty.' He moved towards the bed. 'Look, Jem, I'm so sorry about what's happened. I. . .'

She felt a shutter fold across the window in her mind. 'Oh, don't worry,' she said with a brittleness that belied the hollow anguish lurking deep in her eyes. 'It's more than three weeks now, and I'm just about over it. I've kept myself busy and. . .and. . .it's amazing how. . .' She felt a terrible gulf opening as the momentum of her words slowed and the despair of silence threatened to crush her again. She made a Herculean effort and smiled with what she hoped was bright interest. 'What made you come all the way to Tortola, anyway? I mean, I'm delighted to see you, of course, but. . .' The conversational platitudes sounded hollow to her even as she formed them in her brain.

'I came,' he said, concern deepening his voice, 'because Mrs Stewart rang me in Chiswick two days ago. She said she was worried about you. You weren't eating—weren't sleeping. Just wandering about like a lost thing, and she wanted to know if anyone could come and look after you.' Jem felt the tight reserve spread across her face as he sat down on the end of her bed, gazing at her with unwished for compassion.

'Oh, I don't need looking after,' she said, too brightly. 'Last night I was just. . .well. . .tired. I'm not usually like that.'

'Really?' he muttered sceptically. 'I'm glad! Once was bad enough. You gave me a dreadful scare, Jem. You didn't even recognise me when I arrived. Just sat there staring at me as if I were non-existent.'

She shuddered, not wanting to relive the horrors of the night before, or of all the nights she had spent alone in this silent house for the past three weeks since. . .since. . .Even now her mind refused to form the words that would expose her to the full truth of what had happened. This blank, emotionless state of self-deception was far preferable to the pain she knew would engulf her if she was honest with herself. She closed her mind to what he was saying as he continued.

'At first I thought you'd taken an overdose or something,' he muttered, pacing across the bare, polished boards, 'but then I realised you were just exhausted; mentally and physically spent.' He paused, studying her. 'You need rest and nourishment, young woman, and I'm here to see that you get them. So. . .you lie back there and I'll bring you some breakfast, and then we'll see what we can do with the rest of the day.'

The instant the huge mahogany door had clicked gently behind him she was out of bed, desperate to be up and doing and freed from the trap of his pity. The overwhelming gratitude she had first felt last night, when his voice had penetrated her self-imposed exile from reality, was now being eroded by doubt. As she dressed, in one of the faded cotton frocks still hanging in her wardrobe after four years' absence, she knew that the pit she had been burying herself in for the last three weeks was about to be excavated. Darcy wasn't going to sit back and allow her to wallow in self-pity.

'I wish he hadn't come,' she whispered. The thought of his energy and the merciless insight he had into the workings of her mind disturbed her. 'He knows me too well. He'll poke and probe and bully. He'll try to psychoanalyse me. I can't face going into it all. It's over. There's nothing I can do about it, and I don't want his well-meaning interference.' Her thoughts ricocheted like a demented pinball machine, always just missing the big score of self-revelation.

Flicking a comb through her hair, which was still wet

from the shower, she plastered a glassy smile across her face and went in search of Darcy.

He was in the kitchen, a cavernlike room full of Neanderthal equipment, poking hopelessly through a vast and cumbersome paraffin-operated fridge.

'This kitchen should be donated to a folk museum,' he said, with a kind of awed amusement. 'There's not a single item dated later than 1940. And it all works!' He turned slowly to face her. 'I thought I told you to stay in bed.'

The glassy smile faltered only slightly. 'Oh, I couldn't stay in bed on a beautiful day like this. Look at the sun; look at the sea. Doesn't it make you want to *do* something?' She paced about making frenetic gestures, aware of the exaggerated calm with which he was eyeing her. 'Come along, forget food—let's go for a swim.'

As they moved through the discreet shade of the old wooden house, searching cedar-scented cupboards for towels and swimsuits, she kept up an excitable chatter, laughing shrilly at nothing in particular, wondering how she was going to manage to bring herself down from this plateau of hysteria.

'What do you make of Tamarind Hall, my ancestral home, now that you've seen it for yourself? Is it anything like you imagined from my descriptions?'

'It's better,' he smiled, watching as she feverishly plucked at faded cushions and dusty ornaments, trying to make a permanent imprint of familiar objects on the flesh of her hands. 'You never told me about the light, or the silence, or the smell of two-hundred-year-old wood. . .Or the view.'

He wandered, deliberately slowly, through the open double doors of the entrance hall that served as a spacious, airy sitting-room, and descended the one stone step on to the wide veranda that encircled the house. 'I never expected *this* in a million years.'

'Well, I told you it overlooked the sea, surely?' she said with no little impatience as she followed him.

'Oh, yes,' he said with a grin, 'but not about the colour and clarity of that sea, nor about the islands bobbing on its surface like something out of Robert Louis Stevenson.' He leaned on the rail, peering at them as if he could somehow draw them towards him. 'Hell, the light is so fantastic here I feel as if I could reach out and touch that big one. . .what's it called? "Just" something?'

It was Jem's turn to grin. 'Jost Van Dyke,' she corrected pedantically. 'Named after a Dutch pirate, so they say. Perhaps it *is* a Treasure Island, but I never found any when I used to go there.'

A cloud passed across her eyes as memories of idyllic childhood days intruded briefly. 'But that was a long time ago,' she said with harsh finality. 'Today. . .now. . .is what I shall live for. Come on. Let's have that swim!'

As she set off through the thick undergrowth that had once been a garden and began descending the steep hill to the bay below the house, she began to feel a strange compulsion drawing her. She vaguely heard Darcy behind her crashing through the hydralike plant life as he vainly sought the illusive path she knew instinctively, but the noises of his progress barely impinged. With an irresistible determination she thrust her way through hibiscus, oleander and fleshy, creeping vines that had all reverted to the wild in a mass revolution, very soon finding herself, hot and breathless, emerging on to the crescent of silver sand below the house.

The sun pulsated through the fronds of a sweeping palm as she hastily unfastened her dress, seeing neither the deserted beach nor the diamond-bright clarity of the sea in her haste, and not bothering with the swimsuit she'd brought. When Darcy arrived a few moments later the only sign of Jem was a pathetic little heap of faded clothing discarded on the warm sand as if surplus to some beachcomber's requirements.

The water felt warm and silky against her bare flesh. With easy strokes she cut her way through the rudimentary waves, seeing blearily the shape of Jost Van Dyke and its smaller companions through a film of salt.

Why she felt this sudden need to head towards the islands, she had no idea. She only knew that something was driving her on, and as her arms began to slow and her body to sink imperceptibly lower in the water she neither noticed nor cared that she was gradually pushing herself beyond the limit of her own endurance.

The sun was just cutting itself in two behind the hills of Jost Van Dyke when the last of her flagging strength gave out. She felt strangely aggrieved that she was now probably about to drown. She'd actually swum over to Jost years ago. Why shouldn't she be able to do it today? She rolled over on to her back, exhausted, apathetic, not caring what became of her. And then she saw, out of the corner of her eye, a dark shape moving smoothly towards her through the clear water. With a sudden belated concern for her own safety she kicked out, not sure which way to go.

She felt panic welling up and her toes tingled sharply in anticipation of that illusory snout pursuing her, bumping her, gaping its jaws ready for the kill.

She shrieked in blood-curdling terror as, seconds later, the unspeakable happened and she felt her desperately flailing arm grabbed roughly from behind and she was dragged to a struggling halt. She kicked and fought, a Dervish in mindless fear, until the beast suddenly let out a bellow.

'Jem!' it roared. 'For heaven's sake, calm down. You'll drown us both.'

He towed her, unresisting, back to Tamarind Cove, swimming with the easy grace of an Olympian athlete. They didn't exchange any words until he at last hauled her, naked and demoralised, on to the stiff sand of her own shoreline.

He gazed down at her as she lay, exhausted and gleaming in the embryo moonlight. 'What on earth were you doing?' he demanded harshly, the muscles of his jaw clenching fitfully. 'You could have drowned.'

Jem heaved a sigh and stared bleakly up at the star-spattered sky. 'I know,' she said with lifeless calm. 'I almost think I wanted to.' Wanted to, her brain corrected her, until the moment when she had been faced with the true prospect of death. Then she had realised with overwhelming certainty that dying was the last thing on her agenda.

'That's self-indulgent twaddle,' he hissed, peering down at her from his superior height.

'I know that, too. . .now,' she said with a catch in her voice.

'Well, don't let me hear anything remotely like it again. Do you understand?'

'Yes. . .and. . .' She turned to belatedly thank him for his timely rescue only to find him striding off up the beach for her clothes. Trembling with delayed shock, she struggled to her feet and tottered unsteadily after him, holding out her hands for the thin dress that would afford some semblance of chastity to this wanton exposure.

'I'm sorry,' she murmured brokenly as he handed her her minimal briefs. 'I don't know what——'

'Don't apologise. Rescuing drowning women is a favourite pastime of mine. Especially. . .'

He paused and she raised her glance to his moonlit face, feeling a sudden surge of surprise as she intercepted a strange, glinting expression, instantly hooded by a timely cloud.

She made a grab for her dress, but he swiftly withheld it. 'You can have it once you've made me a solemn promise, Mrs Lister. Will you do that?'

'It depends what it is,' she said suspiciously, trying to quash the sudden feeling of danger that swept through her as the soft breeze from the sea played over her naked breasts like the velvet of a tender touch. 'I don't make promises before I know what I'm letting myself in for.'

'Very wise,' he murmured darkly, 'in the circumstances.'

She felt her trepidation melt into sudden anger. 'Look, I'm very grateful to you for being there. . .for saving me. I honestly don't know what came over me. . .But it doesn't give you the right to dictate salacious terms to me.' The expression in his eyes embarrassed her and she tried to hide her nakedness with outspread hands. 'I am still in my right mind, you know, so I can determine my own affairs. Now, hand me my dress so that we can get back to the house.'

'Not until you promise me that you'll model for me. Like that. Nude.'

That was certainly not the request she had expected.

She stared at him in disbelief for a second, not able to trust her tongue.

'The way you look now. . .' He took a step away from her, scrutinising her avidly. 'With the moon-light—or it could be sunlight, it doesn't matter—highlighting the soft glow of your skin and the subtle curves of that anatomical perfection. . .Well, it would be magic. And with, of course, the landscape here and the purity of the light, I couldn't go wrong.'

She realised as he started to pace about the beach, using her dress to emphasise a point here and there, that he had retreated into his gestating mood. He was no longer conscious of her as Jem. She was a mere body, a collection of skin and bones, a sexless utility.

With a shrug she turned towards the path that led up to the house, not caring now about the leaves brushing her thighs or the warm night air caressing every secret hidey-hole of her flesh. She no longer felt the same constaint, since his eyes had held a different meaning from the one she had assumed. The realisation made her feel oddly flat.

I must be slightly delirious, she thought with a rueful smile, or I wouldn't be enjoying wandering through the bush stark naked.

She was astonished to feel a sense of freedom she hadn't known since arriving back in Tortola three weeks before. She had the impression that some lurking demon had just been purged. By what, she wasn't sure. Could it have been her sudden realisation, out there in the water, of how sweet life was? How foolish to waste any precious second in unnecessary restriction? Perhaps. But she suddenly knew only that she no longer felt hidebound by petty constraints, and that the

thought of modelling for Darcy no longer sent cold
shivers coursing over her.

As she paused on the overgrown path to catch her
breath she turned, spying the gleam of his hair below
her in the moonlight. 'So,' she shouted, abandoning
any last semblance of bashfulness, 'you want to paint
me in the nude? OK. Ready when you are, Mr da
Vinci!'

They lived for three more weeks camping out in Jem's
house on the hill.

Darcy organised a gang of workmen to try to refur-
bish the dilapidation of decades, though Jem insisted
that no modernisation should take place. 'This is how I
like it,' she muttered with prickly fervour. 'This is how
it stays!'

And every day, on the dot of seven, she would follow
Darcy down the veranda steps to the hired Land Rover
and they would set off—up into the mountains, or
along a stretch of deserted coast, or over to the next
large island, Virgin Gorda, for Darcy to indulge his
new passion. Landscape with nude.

The first time she'd had to strip off, contrary to all
her bravado, she *had* found it extremely embarrassing,
but Darcy had been clipped and businesslike.
Detached, as if the sacrifice of her clothes was an
everyday occurrence.

'Good, good,' was all he had said as she'd raised her
hand to unfasten the buttons that reached from breast
to hem of her dusky pink dress. The soft cotton had
slithered down her freckled arms and dropped to the
ground at her feet, leaving her mind feeling as exposed
as the tan of her body. Not daring to look at him, she

had slid her knickers down over her thighs and passively stepped out of them, kicking them aside as if the protection they afforded from the rude outside gaze meant less than nothing to her. Inside she squirmed.

'It's such a strange feeling. Being bare in broad daylight in the middle of a forest.' She had tried to laugh, but her voice trembled and made it sound like a sob. 'I hope nobody comes along!'

He hadn't bothered to comment. 'Just wrap yourself around that tree,' he'd commanded, 'and rest your cheek against it. Right. Lift your leg and cling on like. . .' he manipulated her thigh round the trunk '. . .that. Yes—as if you're making love to the thing. Perfect.' And he had rushed back behind his easel, as excited as a boy with a new train set.

Jem had leaned rather numbly against the bole of the jacaranda, knowing she should be regretting all this and yet realising, deep in her heart, that nothing much mattered now. . .especially not the posturings of her maidenly modesty.

The picture of Darcy's splendidly rounded young models flashed across her mind just as they had marched past her bedroom door. She now knew without a doubt what kind of modelling they did, and she shied away from the invidious comparisons between their ample nakedness and her own. It would be like Rubens' nudes taunting a Modigliani she thought ruefully, and had to smile despite herself.

Gradually, though, she found that posing nude became less traumatic, and she began to almost look forward to the gentle inactivity of her days. She would watch Darcy, spying on the progress of his work, and she realised with amazement that he no longer seemed to mind her watching over his shoulder during her breaks.

'This is beautiful,' she murmured one day, unable to restrain her growing awe. 'The vibrancy that you can conjure from ordinary tubes of paint just seems to be meant for this scenery. Your colours remind me of Gauguin. How do you do it?'

He seemed to be twanging with an inner excitement and his hand flew across the canvas. 'I think I've come of age, Jem. At long last I've realised where I'm going with my painting, and do you know something? It's all due to you.'

'Me?' She stared at him in astonishment, clutching tightly to the flimsy wrap she'd flung on.

'You! When I first met you, your artistic fervour reminded me of my own impassioned youth. I wanted to make sure yours didn't become crippled by disillusioned apathy as mine had, and I thought that helping you to the Maudsby Award was the answer. Well, in a way it was—for me—because you've introduced me to all this. Without you I'd never have come here. I'd have carried on painting stereotyped pictures for braying, mindless vulgarians until anything artistic in me was atrophied and I finally fell into bored self-disgust. Can you imagine? And now, here I am. I've discovered what I've been seeking all these years.'

She turned away, the heaviness in her heart suddenly becoming unbearable. 'I'm glad,' she intoned hoarsely. 'My loss seems to be your gain. At least *something* good's come out of all this.'

'Jem——' He threw down his brush. 'Jem, I'm sorry, I didn't mean to. . .'

She felt remorse cutting through her self-pity. 'Oh, dear, I didn't mean to sound so badly done to.' With an impulsive friendliness submerged by sorrow for the last six weeks she went to him and put her hand on the cool brown of his arm. 'I have tried, Darcy. I've. . .I've tried to forget. To behave as if nothing's happened. I nearly managed to put it out of my mind, and yet. . .'

The concern in his eyes made her falter, unable to carry on in case the strait-jacket she'd strapped around her emotions burst in a welter of messy pathos. She turned away. 'You've been very good to me. Very patient and understanding. Thank you.'

That evening she descended the overgrown path to the bay carrying a small wooden box. Darcy followed at a discreet distance.

The night was impossibly still as she leaned on a rock beside an insignificant little waterfall whose stream cut shallow furrows in the sand as it abased itself to its master the sea.

She paused to watch as the huge orange globe of the sun dipped its salute to the horizon, sending a shimmering path of fire slithering across the sea to her feet. But she was inured to nature's extravagance by the compelling purpose that had drawn her to this spot, and she barely noticed the flamboyance of colour in the sky, or the unnatural silence that hung in the air. Flame and crimson streaked across huge navy anvil-headed clouds. The birds and insects were mute. A storm was imminent.

'I shall scatter her ashes here,' Jem heard herself say in a small, dead voice and, as the exhibitionist of the solar system finally doused itself in the bromide of the sea, she released the lid of the box and trickled its contents over the gurgling water.

The storm came in the night. A fearsome wind clutched at the house, ripping and pummelling it in fury. Rain and unripe mangoes lashed the roof. Through the warped planks in the front door shutters glimpses of lunatic branches could be seen flailing back and forth, and an occasional bush, torn out by the roots, sent scudding across the littered ground.

It was after midnight, when nature was reaching a pitch of discordance to rival a modern composer, that Jem cried out.

Darcy was in her room, fading torch flickering dimly, before the second scream had barely passed her lips.

'Grandma!' she cried, her head rolling fitfully over the pillow. 'Grandma, where are you?'

'Jem.' He shook her firmly. 'Jem, wake up!'

Her eyes flew open. 'Where is she?' she mumbled disjointedly, trying to sit up. 'I can't find her.'

Darcy swallowed, unable to find an answer.

'I dreamed I was in the house in Stoke Newington, and Ali got out into the yard. Gran. . .Grandma was there, and she went to save him, but the dogs started howling and shrieking, and when I looked I couldn't see her. I. . .They'd. . .they. . .' She looked at him with a sudden bleakness. 'She's dead. I've lost her.'

He sighed, knowing that at last she had accepted. At last her mind had shaken off the amnesiac cotton wool that she had wrapped it in and come to terms with the truth. Her grandmother was dead.

'Yes, Jem. She died peacefully, in no pain, they told me.'

'But I was too late. She didn't know me. By the time I got to the hospital she was in a coma.' She lay back, the first slow tears beginning to well up in her eye corners. 'There was so much I wanted to say. I tried to tell her that I could take care of her, she needn't work any more. I tried, oh, I did try to tell her that I loved her, but. . .but she didn't hear.'

A huge sob hauled itself out of her chest. 'All the wonderful things she did for me, and now I'll never be able to repay her. I wanted to do so much. Oh, Darcy, she looked so frail and alone.'

With a howl of anguish as old as mankind she buried her face in the pillow and allowed her inadequacies to be wrenched out of her in great rasping sobs. Pain and loss swept over her. She felt the eternal unfairness of death filling her with impotent resentment, making her want to hit out at life.

'Why her?' she shouted into the pillow, drumming her fists. 'She didn't deserve it. Why? Why? Why?'

Gradually she felt her anger subside and a forlorn realisation of her aloneness took over. 'What am I going to do, Darcy?' she murmured, barely audible above the shriek of the wind.

He took her hand. 'You're going back to college, to carry on with that wonderful work you've been doing,' he said, deliberately shelving the deeper, more profoundly disturbing meaning behind her words. 'After we've got the house organised we'll be off back to London.'

She nodded, incapable as yet of encompassing it.

'And then we'll see where——'

An almighty crash ripped through the house. Light poured into every corner of the room, exposing them in bald whiteness, and then was gone. The walls shook and the heavy, oppressive furniture, familiar and unremarkable throughout her childhood, looked now like monsters in some hideously exaggerated Sendak opera set.

In the half-second that this phenomenon had taken,

Jem had hurled herself, like a quarter-back, straight into Darcy's waiting arms.

Fear clutched at her heart. She was comforted by the feel of his strong arms enfolding her and his hands soothingly stroking her hair. The sound of his voice lulled her, even though the words were lost in the clamour from outside.

She lifted her face to him just as he brought his down to look at her. Their cheeks brushed; their noses bumped; their lips met.

She felt his chest muscles tauten as his arms tightened around her, trapping her. Feeling drained and snuffly, she moved her face away from his, but she didn't move out of his arms. Instead, she began to tremble in response to the thudding of his heart. She knew it wasn't fear that was tripping his pulse, just as she knew that the fear she was feeling was no longer anything to do with the weather. It was a delicious fear.

With infinite delicacy he pressed her back on to the pillow and, as the first pearly light crept through the window, which had been denuded of its shutters in the fearsome blast, he gazed down on her tousled disarray.

'I. . .' he began, but she reached up a hand to his lips, her eyes huge with understanding.

She felt his hands grasp hold of the old, flimsy cotton of her nightdress. With one movement he'd ripped it apart, exposing the alabaster length of her.

As his burning eyes drank their fill she lay, paralysed by inadequacy. She felt almost apologetic, absurdly so, not realising in her self-deprecation the electrifying picture she presented with her satin skin and perfect, long-limbed grace. All she could think of was the ugliness of her tears and the guilt of wanting him so badly at this most inappropriate of times.

He was very gentle. She felt the flutter of his breath as he kissed her swollen eyelids. 'You are so beautiful,' he whispered, running an exploratory finger over her stomach. 'I want to paint you like this.'

And then there were no more words. There was only sensation. Perfect, achingly sweet. His lips and hands creating sublime torment, the cool velvet of his skin a burst of curling desire.

The storm was programmed to self-destruct in the same instant that Jem's rhythmical moans became one sudden animal cry. Both element and woman subsided with a dying moan, spent.

She lay, crushed by Darcy's weight, fighting down a bubble of euphoric laughter. So this was what it felt like to be a woman. She had no substance. She was pure animus.

As he rolled away from her in the gloom she lay spread-eagled, all shyness gone, feline, sated. A fine tracery of regret began to slowly besiege her. She shouldn't have grabbed at this pleasure while still mourning such an unbearable loss. How heartless she felt. And yet. . .the tingle that still lingered invalidated reproach.

'Darcy?' she whispered softly, stroking her hand across his thigh. 'Darcy, I feel. . .oh. . .' She wanted to find words profound enough to express the deep fulfilment he had brought her, but they all seemed too hackneyed. She kissed the hollow between his shoulders instead.

He stirred, swinging his legs over the side of the bed and retrieving his robe in one fluid movement. 'I know, I know!' His voice raked her with its harshness. 'Hell, what have I done? I must have been mad. It was like taking sweets from a baby.'

The bottom slowly fell out of Jem's lustrous new world. With a lurch of pain that made her feel physically sick, she realised she wasn't the only one to feel guilt at what they'd just done, only his was for the living. The long, poisonous finger of Venetia had reached out to them, even here. The hurt Venetia would feel from a distance weighed more heavily with him than the suffering he was inflicting on Jem herself from so close.

He deliberately turned his back. 'It really will have to be divorce now.' His voice sounded rough. 'I had hoped, if your British nationality had come through before the year was up, that we could have been granted an annulment. . .but now. . .we're going to have to wait it out.' He glanced at her briefly, a curious expression disfiguring his face, a mixture of anger and pain, regret and something else, something deep and unfathomable that Jem was afraid to try to interpret in case it inflicted more hurt upon what she was already going through.

'You mean. . .' she faltered, 'You mean you've only been waiting for me to be granted British nationality, and then you were going to divorce me?' For some reason the word 'divorce' came out sounding tight and husky. It wasn't surprising, though, she reflected dismally. The possible end of her marriage to this man had been increasingly thrust into the darkest, most inaccessible corner of her mind, a dreadful thing, never to be imagined. And it was only now, as she stared up in horror at the impassive back of her newly gained, but oh, so swiftly lost lover, that she realised why. She was deeply, hopelessly, irrevocably in love with him.

How slowly it had crept up on her, this feeling, this certainty. The wondrous excitement, the longing to be forever near him, the nervous pleasure she derived from pleasing him, all those things that she now realised without a doubt had grown and expanded into acute, terminal adoration.

His voice, tense and hoarse, cut through the miasma of pain that filled her mind. 'No!' He sounded exasperated. 'You've *got* to be married a whole year before you can petition for divorce nowadays—I thought even you would know that!' He ran his hand through the quicksilver of his hair and groaned. 'You really did trust me, didn't you? I was going to parade you before a solicitor and cite non-consummation of the marriage as grounds for annulment and it would have taken just a glance at you with your naïveté, your virtuousness, for him to have believed me implicitly. . .But now. . .One look at that radiance and I'd be laughed to scorn.'

She stared mutely at him, unable to speak.

'Hell, I'm being a bastard!' he cried suddenly, lifting the sheet and carefully hiding her nakedness. 'I'm sorry.' His voice dropped, low and concerned. 'I didn't hurt you too much, did I?'

She hadn't known that she was crying. She felt the tears now as they ran down and made cold puddles inside her ears. She felt utterly demoralised. She knew that there was no answer.

CHAPTER NINE

THREE days after the shattering blow of Darcy's rebuff had embedded shrapnel deep within her, Jem returned with him to London.

Why, she was hard-pressed to explain to herself. The dull ache of her bereavement seemed almost frivolous compared to the overwhelming pain of the newly awakened love she felt for Darcy. Yet I'd rather have that pain than the emptiness of being without him, she thought, with woebegone masochism.

And there was to be no compromise in his exclusion of her from his life and his plans. She knew with a desperate finality that, though he had been kind and gentle, thoughtful and distantly polite since telling her so brutally about their imminent divorce, his mind was made up. His heart lay elsewhere. . .in the brash and glittery world of Venetia Pitt.

Back in Chiswick she found that living with him was torture. She wondered constantly how she could bring herself to awaken every morning to the knowledge that the man she was dippy about cared slightly less for her than he did for his ragamuffin dog. And also that the time was fast approaching when his self-appointed obligation would be fulfilled and he would tell her to leave and start the separation period, or even ask her to divorce him right away.

Each time Jem saw that word in her mind's eye she recoiled. Not only from the inevitability of the dreaded parting, but also from the regret she felt at all those

wasted chances she'd let slip through her grasp. She'd
had so much time to woo him, if she'd only known how
deeply he'd insinuated himself under her skin. But now
there was no time left.

Eventually she found she had counterfeited so many
transparent excuses in her desperate need to be close
to him 'for one last time' that she was convinced he
must be feeling surfeited by her mooning presence. It
came as a sick relief, therefore, to be accosted one
Saturday afternoon as she made her languid way into
her studio and dealt the knock-out punch.

'Ah, Jem,' he said distantly, staring over her head.
'Come into the study a moment, will you?'

It was a command. At last it had come. He wanted
her to leave. She trooped after him, heart thumping a
Zulu beat, and stood blinking in the rays of the sun as
he walked over to the window and looked out on the
bleak twigs of February. Ali was padding across the
grass in lumbering pursuit of a street-wise robin, and
Jem reflected absently that perhaps she ought to leave
him behind, he was obviously so at home here. But as
she braced herself for the blow of Darcy's dismissal,
and the Oscar-winning performance she was going to
have to contrive to simulate indifference, the phone
shrilled loudly on the roll-top desk between them.

Darcy turned, a glower of impatience clouding his
features. 'Hell!' he muttered explosively, snatching up
the receiver. 'Yes?' he barked savagely into it, and
then paused for a disconcertingly long time, drawing
jagged doodles among a litter of papers.

He turned slightly, seeming to be trying to exclude
Jem, but as she moved with relief to leave he waved
her back.

'Venetia, I thought we'd gone into all that,' he said

with sudden irritability. 'The wedding can wait a little longer, surely? You've hung on this long, what's a few more months? It can wait till after we get back. . .I know, darling,' he said silkily, obviously riding rough-shod over whatever argument she was proposing, 'but a three-month lecture tour of twenty US states is not the time or the place to be thinking of weddings. Later, love, later.' And without another word he replaced the receiver, cutting off the birdlike squawks of Venetia's cajolery.

Jem was grateful for the chair behind her knees. A sudden wave of dizziness struck her, and a sick despair made her legs buckle under her. No amount of acting could have disguised the sheer horror on her face, and she could only thank heaven that Darcy had stridden across to the window once more and seemed less interested in her than in the stark branches of a lilac bush tapping at the glass.

'Well, that wasn't quite the way I envisaged telling you,' he said after what seemed like forever. 'Venetia's arranged a whirlwind lecture tour for me in America. . .much against my will, I hasten to add. . .so I shall be away for three months from tomorrow. Will you be able to cope?'

He still had his back to her and, despite the misery coursing through her from her enforced eavesdropping, she sensed a strange kind of regret in him. Almost as if, despite his imminent divorce from her and marriage to the triumphant Venetia, he was loath to part with her.

With lifeless calm she spoke. 'I thought you'd prefer me to leave, under the circumstances.'

'No. . .whatever made you think that? There's

Nathan, for one thing. There'd be nobody to look after him.'

Ah, so that was it. 'Your mother could have him.'

'He prefers you!'

'He lacks discrimination.'

Darcy turned and smiled at her, a weary, preoccupied smile that sent her jittery with yearning protectiveness. He looked tired, the fine lines round his eyes white against the still-burnished tan. His decision had not been cheap, obviously.

'*I* prefer you. My mother is fond of him, but she forgets to exercise him. He'd get fat! I'm ashamed to realise that you're the one who's taken him out every day since we got back from. . .from Tortola.' He was doodling distractedly again. 'I've been very neglectful.'

'I enjoyed it.' This barren politeness was rubbing Jem's new hurt into raw blisters of pain. 'So. . .I'm to stay here and hold the fort till you get back, is that it?'

'Yes. . .I. . .' He looked at her with sudden frankness. 'Look, I know the situation between us here has become impossible, and I'd made up my mind to broach it with you this weekend, but then Venetia sprang this lecture tour on me last night—some other client of hers is ill and can't go—so we'll sort everything out when I get back. But you'll stay in the meantime? I'm counting on you.'

Quietly she nodded, defeated by his openness. He had been going to tell her everything. That, because he wanted to marry Venetia, he wanted her to begin divorce proceedings as soon as possible. In any case, she would have to go. It was no longer right that they should be living in the same house. But now that he was going away and had a use for her he wouldn't throw her out. . .just yet!

'I've organised money for you with my bank, and made a list of appropriate phone numbers should anything go wrong. Mrs Murgatroyd will come in as usual, to——'

'Keep an eye on me!'

'—to clean, and Venetia's secretary will be able to get in touch with me if anything drastic happens.'

'Her secretary? Where's Venetia going to be?' Even as she bluntly formed the words, with heartsick certainty she knew the answer.

'Also in America. She's there now doing some last-minute organising. That was her phoning from New York.'

'Oh. . .I see.' That was what it meant. The final nail was hammered into the coffin of her hopes. Venetia and Darcy together for three months. By the end of that time the legal year would be up on the marriage, and the divorce proceedings could be well under way. It occurred to her that, since Venetia didn't know her beloved Darcy was already married, she was probably angling for a Reno job, the fitting end to a gruelling tour shepherding Darcy ever further into total dependence on her. But he obviously couldn't give in yet. He was putting her off until he was a free man. But she would work on him while they were away together, and Jem had no doubt that by the time they returned she would be thrown out with the rubbish.

Darcy was still talking, giving her instructions, but she wasn't listening. A new determination had taken hold of her. She would not allow herself the humiliation of such a possibility. Before he came back and asked her to, she would start to divorce him on grounds of unreasonable behaviour, as he'd originally suggested. After all, he wouldn't contest it, he'd said.

Pain at the thought of such an action lay like a bunched fist in her breast, but she knew there was no going back. A life spent with Darcy was obviously a figment of her fevered imagination. . .but how she was going to cope with life without him was something she shied away from even contemplating.

'Jem, I'm speaking to you!' His voice broke through the barrier of her gloom. 'Has the money from Tamarind Hall come through yet?'

She raised huge amber eyes, veiled by the need to retain some dignity, to his querying blue ones.

'Tamarind Hall?' What was he referring to? 'Oh, yes. . .of course. . .yes, I got the first payment last week.'

She supposed it was natural that he should be concerned whether the rent he'd organised for her house just before they left Tortola was arriving. As long as her new tenant paid up promptly she would have a reasonable source of income, and Darcy need then feel no further responsibility for her. He could cast her off with impunity.

'That's it, then. Everything's organised. I'll be leaving very early in the morning, so don't bother to see me off. You look as if you could do with the sleep.'

She felt dowdiness engulf her with his concern. She didn't want his sympathy. It seemed so unfair that the only time he noticed her was when her need for him had reduced her to apathetic ugliness. Pining was a curse on the looks.

It took her a long time to adjust to the silence. After daytimes spent in art school clamour she found the nights in the big, empty, soundless house after Darcy had gone unnerving. Faint echoes of the operas he'd

listened to so often mooned through the dark recesses.
Madam Butterfly seeking her Pinkerton across the hall;
Isolde swearing undying love to Tristan drifting
through the study and up the stairs, and the tragic
strains of *Traviata* following her everywhere she ventured. She realised with a pang how melancholy his
choice had been recently. Perhaps being trapped in a
barren marriage had jaundiced him!

And weekends seemed to drag unconscionably.
Nathan's walks helped to pass the time, either at
Palladian Chiswick House or further afield in the wide
open spaces of Gunnersbury Park, but she always had
to return to the stillness of a house overpoweringly
pervaded by the spirit of the man she loved so
hopelessly.

She did receive one slight fillip about three weeks
after Darcy had left. She was at long last granted
British nationality. But once she had paid her fee and
sworn her Oath of Allegiance she realised, with a
sinking despair, that the last tenuous reason for clinging
on to marriage with Darcy had been tweaked out from
under her.

And then, one morning, a new and awful truth began
to seep into her subconscious. As she came downstairs
to let Ali and Nathan out for their morning saraband
around the shrubbery, before she could reach the
kitchen door a devastating bout of nausea overtook her
and she found herself hanging on to the kitchen sink,
heaving her heart up.

That evening she let herself into the dead house and,
without bothering to switch on any lights, she quietly
walked across the familiar hall and up the two flights
of stairs that led to Darcy's studio. Tentatively she
turned the knob, half expecting to find the door locked

against her, but the latch snapped loudly in the silence and the door swung inwards, exposing the huge, moon-lit room in stark display. She crept across the creaky boards, pausing to gaze at the half-finished still life propped on his easel, and then made her way wearily to the chaise-longue under the giant window.

Lying there, mind in neutral, horror at her imposs-ible situation forced well into the background, she gazed sightlessly through the blank glass away to infinity. The stars belittled her, so knowing, so perma-nent, and yet, when Ali found her and thrust his importunate muzzle under her chin, his affectionate touch only reinforced how gargantuan was the problem facing her.

Yes. . .she might be just a mere speck in the universe whose life was of no great shakes in the eventual order of things, but to the tiny unborn scrap that was even now growing inside her she was the most important person alive.

CHAPTER TEN

AGAINST her will the details insinuated themselves through Jem's subconscious. Eight weeks, the doctor had said, handing her a confusing bundle of leaflets. 'Eight weeks, Miss Selby. What will your boyfriend think of all this?' What, indeed?

It wasn't until she had found herself outside in the bitter night that she'd realised she'd not even thought to give the receptionist her married name. So brief was the time left to enjoy that status, she'd automatically resumed thinking of herself as single.

That must be why the leaflets on breast care and exercises, diet and varicose veins included a short treatise on abortion and the invitation to phone if advice was needed.

Her mind recoiled. The stars, deep-frozen into the cloudless blackness, mocked her now through the panes of Darcy's window. What would her boyfriend think? What could he think? What could she possibly tell him?

He'd be in Washington now, fêted, lionised. The Pitts would be in close attendance, making herself indispensable, flattering, oiling round him, sharing the limelight, dropping deadly insinuations about 'that girl' he'd left in his house, ingratiating herself ever further into his affections, smoothing the way to her goal. . .his name and his love. Against opposition like that, Jem knew she stood no chance.

She *could* tell him, she supposed. Use her undeniable

ace to keep him tied to her. The unwilling husband compromised into perpetual marriage. The vision of his anger and bafflement sent arrowheads glancing against her ribs. That he would honour his duty she had no doubt. That he would hate her for it for the rest of his life she knew with a bitter certainty that caught at her breath with the jagged fingers of suffocation.

But he would be bound to find out, even if she just meekly petitioned for divorce, as he wanted, and said nothing. He would see her at college resembling a barrage balloon. It wouldn't take him long to realise why, and then what would he do?

But surely, she thought, she could lie? No need to admit anything. Perhaps she could even name some other man. Improbabilities stacked themselves around her mind like supermarket shelving. He wouldn't want to know, anyway. He'd be too relieved at having got rid of her to ask dangerous questions.

And she would have enough money. No need to be financially beholden to him. The rent from Tamarind Hall was more than adequate, plus her scholarship, and, after the baby was born. . .She caught her breath. Yes, she really was going to have Darcy's baby. A fragile life. A tenuous link between the two of them. A perpetual manifestation of her love that would burn forever for this hateful, infuriating, divine man.

The abortion leaflet slipped from her lap and floated under the chaise-longue. Not even the faintest ripple of conjecture had crossed her mind on that subject. There was not the remotest chance of her willingly giving up the life of this baby. It was hers. It was his. She would have it and fiercely protect it. Her cold hands caressed the startling flatness of her stomach beneath her coat. It's funny, she thought, how fate

offers quirky compensations. She might have lost
Darcy, but she had been allowed the next best thing.
His child.

The phone beside her bed rang piercingly. She groped
for the light and mumbled something incoherent into
the mouthpiece.

'Jem?' The voice sounded tinny and small, but the
unmistakable timbre sent firecrackers exploding in her
veins, bringing her wide awake instantly.

'Sorry I'm a bit overdue. I had some things to attend
to.' A *frisson* of panic crawled over her skin as she
tried not to imagine what those 'things' could be. 'We'll
be catching Concorde in a couple of hours, and should
be back at Heathrow this morning local time. Check
the time for me and come and pick us up in the car,
will you?. . .Jem?'

The transatlantic silence rang in her ear. It had
arrived at last. The day she had been dreading for
three long months. Leaving day. The fearful anticipation was over.

'Yes,' she croaked, barely audible across the room,
let alone three thousand miles. 'Yes, I'll be there.' And
with a shaking hand she lowered the receiver.

She dressed mechanically, packing the last few of
her belongings into her meagre luggage as she finished
with them, dragging herself downstairs and went
through the motions of eating breakfast. The question
of what she should do about her precious sculptures
drifted through her mind, but it seemed far too great a
problem to tackle now. 'Oh, leave them,' the defeatist
in her said, knowing full well that she'd regret it almost
at once.

Nathan seemed to sense her suffering, and instead of

his usual headlong tug he trotted demurely by her side through the awakening streets. London smelled fresh and expectant, and the May breeze ruffled Jem's hair, but as she gazed into the sky at the jets lumbering past one a minute, stacking over Chiswick for the run into Heathrow, the chill of midwinter settled on her heart. Another few hours and it would be them up there.

The phone rang again when she got back to the house, but the leap her pulse made was wasted. He'd be circling the Statue of Liberty at this moment, preparatory to setting off at twice the speed of sound for England. No, it was only Mr Morris of Morris, Jenkins and Co to query a couple of points on her divorce application.

'Your husband has not replied to our letter yet, Mrs Lister.'

She fingered the large buff envelope addressed to Darcy on the desk in front of her. 'No, he's still away. He's due back today. I'm sure he'll be in touch very soon.'

She paused, remembering the look of discreet surprise on Mr Morris's face as she had filed her suit on what should have been a celebration day. Their first anniversary. 'He'll be only too delighted,' she had murmured brokenly.

All too soon the time came to leave for the airport. The car, loaned to her during his absence but seldom used, felt unfamiliar, and she was grateful for the need for dogged concentration over the switchback of the Chiswick flyover and through the wolf-pack of the motorway.

She parked the Morgan in the car park and made her way, with blenching heart, to Terminal Four. She stood within sight of the Concorde gate, glancing at the arrivals monitor to confirm that it had landed. Any second now he should emerge.

Nervously she ticked off the arrangements she had made. She'd go back to the house with him, collect her bags and then go into college until she could decently lumber herself on to Yvonne and Mike. They'd told her she could stay with them until the tiny flat she'd rented was vacant, but she didn't like to impose herself on them too soon.

Her mind jittered round and round, trying to concentrate and yet finding that visions of Darcy kept intruding. How would he look after so long? Would she even know him? Her mind's image of him was so blurred now from over-exposure that she wondered if she would walk straight past him, purblind.

She wrapped her baggy coat a little more tightly round herself—for disguise against imagined swelling as much as from the chill of nerves—and was just about to take a turn around the crowded terminal to relieve the tension when there was a slight flurry of activity and a star-burst of flashbulbs by the gate. 'Darcy Lister' said a well-bred voice, and two or three gossip column hacks hove to alongside their living bread and butter, pummelled him briefly with impertinent questions, and then retired to pounce on other prey. He emerged, tall and elegant, white hair flopping over one eye, expensive jeans barely creased, and held out his arm towards a radiant Venetia pushing her way through the throng from behind. He smiled down at her fondly and tucked her arm through his.

Jem backed away, panic clawing at her throat. They mustn't see her. She must escape. She turned to run, unaware of where she was going, just conscious that she had to get as far as possible from the aura of their love. It spilled out of Venetia with indecent profusion, suffocating and cloying.

It wasn't until Jem found herself beside the taxi-rank, ordering the driver to take her to Chiswick and then point east, that she saw again, in her mind's eye, the hand that so eagerly clutched Darcy's sleeve. Slim and pale, the red nails clawing at the rich leather of his jacket and displaying a diamond huge enough to flash its message half-way across the world. . .'He's mine. Lay off!'

She wondered briefly how they'd get home as she laid the car park ticket prominently on the hall table. Darcy would be very angry with her for leaving him to struggle with taxis. And so would Venetia! Jem allowed herself a momentary satisfaction before handing the taxi-driver her case and looking round for one last time at this house that had been her home for so long. The ache she felt was like the anger and rejection after her grandmother's death. An emptiness that no amount of activity could fill. A death, in a way. Stubbornly she wiped the tears from her cheeks. She wouldn't give in. She would just collect Ali and go. Out of the life of Darcy Lister forever.

But Ali was not to be collected. He'd vanished. Desperately she searched, knowing that time was running out and that they could arrive at any moment, furious and accusing, or worse, forgiving and impossibly understanding. But all in vain. At last, with the taxi's meter turning cartwheels, she abandoned the search, telling herself that he'd be quite safe for a little longer, and that when the coast was clear and Darcy had gone out one day she'd return and collect him. With trembling limbs and pounding heart she ran down the path and bundled herself into the seat of the cab.

'Never mind, it might never 'appen,' said the professionally cheery chappie from the front. 'Where to?'

'Anywhere!' she cried despairingly. 'Just get me away from this house.' And as the vehicle lurched out into the road she crouched back in the corner and gave in to the weary sobs of disillusion.

She'd found a flat south of the river. The attic of a house belonging to a third-year student at college, and for the two rooms, kitchen and a shared bathroom she was paying less than for the single glory-hole in Stoke Newington. She could have been happy there. Indeed, she tried. The flat was pleasant, as were the co-tenants of the house, the area round about was agreeable, the weather couldn't have been better for the time of year. . .and yet. . .and yet. . .the sorrow that was lodged like a nuclear reactor deep in her heart permeated her every waking moment with hopelessness.

She tried to look forward, to plan for the birth of her baby with positiveness, but everything she started, like the painting of the tiny room earmarked as nursery, or trips to the shops to buy mundane objects like maternity bras the size of a hammock, all fizzled out. There seemed to be no point to it all. Who was there to care what she did or how she looked? Her grandmother was dead, and the one living person to whom she would have been proud to show off her new home, and who would have appreciated her wry comments on its décor, was the self-same who had sent her helter-skelter in need of the solitude that now oppressed her night and day. 'I have spread my dreams under your feet,' Yeats had written, but as she sat among the meagre furniture and gazed around she felt the hobnails of fate grinding those dreams into dust.

By the time she had screwed up the courage to return

to Chiswick for Ali, she had still not set foot in the
college. The prospect of coming face to face with Darcy
was too devastating. Instead, she had tried to work at
home, but she seemed to have no power over her
hands. They drew or sculpted Darcy no matter what
her brain told them to do. She began to feel trapped in
the claustrophobia of obsession. She clung desperately
to the hope that when she eventually collected Ali it
would lift the curse of these compulsions. That she
would be free from the dread of unexpected meetings.
Able to begin her life anew on her own terms.

So it was with a substantial dash of bravado that she
issued forth on the gruelling journey by train and tube
to Chiswick. It was a Tuesday—the day he taught at
the college—so she felt reasonably safe.

The key to the house made a painful imprint on the
palm of her hand, and her heart thumped disconcertingly as she trudged up the long road from Turnham
Green station. It took her an age to decide whether
Darcy really was out, but as the car was nowhere in
sight and the garage door wide open she eventually
screwed up enough courage to creep, disguised as a
passing rain cloud, up the garden path and in through
the front door.

Ali came to greet her immediately, yeowling
piteously. 'Oh!' she cried, scooping him up and burying
her face in his fur. 'You great big adorable softy. How
I've missed you!'

'I'm flattered!' drawled an all too familiar voice from
behind her. 'I did have the unworthy feeling you were
trying to avoid me.'

For an instant the world stopped turning. That voice!
That unmistakable intonation! The shock of hearing
him again after so long froze her to the floor. With a

sinking dread she realised she would have to turn and face him, and in the hours that it seemed to take all the aching months of missing him flashed before her.

But nothing could prepare her for the impact of seeing him again, so close. He seemed bigger somehow, more vital, and the blue of his eyes sparkled against the copper of his tan. She couldn't speak. He took her breath away. He was more beautiful in the flesh than any of the images she'd projected on to the blank wall of her memory. She revelled in the half-forgotten details of his quirky mouth, his long, flexible fingers, forgetting for a second the dreary truth. That this was a snatched, illicit delight.

The front door clicked shut. Darcy leaned his slender length lazily against the frame, folding his arms in expectation of enlightenment. Jem felt menaced suddenly, brought down to earth by his sheer physical presence. Desperately, she looked round, trying to find an escape, but the glint in his eye told her she was out of luck.

'I won't ask where you've been. That would smack too strongly of the heavy husband! Perhaps I should just say "welcome home".'

'I shouldn't bother.' Anxiety made her contentious. 'I'm not staying.'

'Ah, you were merely passing and thought you'd drop in to find out how I was? How considerate. . .Well, I'm fine. My index finger is a little sore from all the phoning I've been doing on your behalf, and I'm afraid my car had to have an early service due to excess mileage chasing up clues about you. But, all in all, I'm well, thank you. And you? Blooming, I see.'

Hastily she clutched her jacket across her proud little bulge, exaggerated by Ali's weight dragging on her dress, confident that it was only obvious to a practised eye. 'Oh, I. . .I'm fine,' she said airily to hide the puzzlement she felt by his efforts to run her to earth. Why could he possibly have wanted to find her so urgently? What solecism had she committed? With a quick, false smile she tried to block any more of his sarcasm. 'Look, I'm sorry about dashing off the way I did, but I suddenly had the chance of this flat and I couldn't let it——'

'At Heathrow Airport?' He unpropped himself from the door and advanced towards her. 'Someone fleeing the country tossed you the key in passing, did they, so you abandoned me to my fate and a fruitless two-hour search for you? Unkind, dear Jem, cruel! I fear Venetia was not best pleased.'

At the mention of that name Jem whipped round, realising her danger. Venetia! She'd forgotten. Where was she?

'She's not here, don't panic. At work, probably. Look, I'd be grateful if you'd at least come into the kitchen and have a coffee or something. I find these extempore chats in the hall unsettling.' With his hand deceptively light on her shoulder he led her along the passage.

The kitchen. Venetia's new domain. But, looking round tentatively, Jem was surprised how little she had changed it. Even the rude caricature she herself had drawn of Darcy was still impaled by its rusty drawing-pin to the peg-board. It puzzled her. Surely that would be the first thing a new broom, that particular new broom, would sweep away? She couldn't be living here yet. Not until after they were married, obviously. Jem relaxed perceptibly. Now at least there was only Darcy to contend with.

She watched him covertly as he prowled about, confident in the familiar role of coffee-preparer for the two of them. It felt almost homely, dangerously so, back in the well-remembered domesticity. She told herself to snap out of this fatal complacency. In ten minutes it would all be over. She'd be out on the street. She drew in a breath, desperate to assert herself, even if only to refuse his coffee, when he looked up innocently and blandly enquired, 'When is the baby due?'

If she hadn't been leaning heavily against the table, Jem would have fallen over. He couldn't possibly know. She'd not told anyone. The bump hardly showed. Trawling in her scattered wits, she clutched the table with both hands. 'Baby? W-what do you mean? I'm not having a baby.' She knew she didn't sound very convincing.

'I didn't say that you were. I just wanted to know if you knew who was. And by your reaction. . .I think you do!'

'I don't understand. What are you talking about?' she blurted, desperately playing for time.

'Well. . .to need an abortion, I assume you have to be pregnant first.' He turned to get mugs from the cupboard beside the sink. 'And I was just wondering who it was who'd been jettisoning lurid leaflets on the subject under my modelling couch. I worked it out that it could only be you! No one else has been near my studio since before Christmas.'

Stunned to the point of speechlessness, Jem could only stare back at him, the anguish of her soul mirrored in the amber of her eyes.

'And if that's the case,' he ploughed on remorselessly, 'what's all this damn fool nonsense about filing for divorce? I had that little bombshell waiting for me as well when I eventually got home.' He was moving dangerously close to her, and the mesmerism in his voice was lulling her brain into something resembling chocolate mousse.

'Why shouldn't I divorce you?' She struggled against the opium of his nearness, willing her brain to function. 'What if I am pregnant? My baby's no business of yours.'

'It is if it happens to be mine.'

The sudden harshness in his voice frightened her more than the grip of his hands on her shoulders. Struggling under the dual pressures of fear and guilt she spat out, with far greater venom than she intended, 'It's not yours. It's not your baby.'

She felt an odd kind of disloyalty to her baby as she uttered the words. Darcy *was* the father, and she knew she should acknowledge that for the baby's sake, but somehow the denials kept pouring out.

'And it wouldn't make any difference even if it were. I'm quite capable of having a baby and looking after it without your good name to back me up. Marriage isn't a prerequisite to bearing children, you know.'

'No. . .but it helps!'

'I told you, I don't want your help. I want you to just get out of my life and let me make my own mistakes in peace.'

He let go of her, and as she slumped against the table she wondered by what dreary inevitability the situation had reached this nadir.

'Is that really what you want?' His voice held an edge. Dread, she thought, listening keenly. Fear that she might, even now, try to appeal to his sense of honour and beg him to stand by her.

With her chin tilted proudly, she nodded. 'Yes, of course.'

'Well, then, if it's not my baby, whose in hell is it?'

She took a deep breath, not knowing until the words were out what she was going to say. 'It was. . .a boy at a party. . .while you were away. I got drunk. I didn't know. . .' The lies tumbled over themselves to escape. 'And, in any case,' she laughed falsely, 'I don't know why we're getting so worked up. I did have that abortion, you know.' Once she'd started she seemed incapable of stopping.

'What?'

'Oh, yes, about two weeks ago.' She couldn't believe that these crazy words were really coming from her. After all, he'd know all too soon that they just weren't true. But then, maybe after all it wasn't so bad, because after the divorce there'd be very little he could do apart from watch her grow bigger. And he'd be safely married to Venetia by then. 'That's why I haven't been into college. I. . .well. . .I wasn't feeling too good.'

'I'm sorry about that.' His response sounded mechanical, as if he had ceased to concern himself with her problems. 'I wouldn't know about you not being at college. I've done my term. My contract was only until Christmas, so I'm a slave to life class no more.'

Relief and huge sadness swept over her. So that was why he was at home. It also meant that he was about to step out of her life completely. After the divorce she could return to college free from the suspense of bumping into him round every corner, of being found out in her huge lie. But her life would be predictable and empty. Thrill-less; Darcyless.

'But. . .' He was still talking. She focused on his mouth, lipreading frantically as a temporary buzzing in her ears blotted out the sound of his voice. 'But that doesn't mean I've just abandoned all responsibility for you. You're a mere baby yourself. I can't just cast you out into the world like this.'

'Oh, please! Don't have a conscience about me,' she cried bitterly. 'I'm a bit of flotsam that caught your eye, but now it's time to chuck me back into the mainstream again. I've got my life. You've got yours. Don't let's impede each other any more. We've served our own purposes with each other. Now's the time to quit. Amiably. With no fuss. I'm a British citizen now, so they won't throw me out or anything, so you see, there's no reason to stay together now.' Her voice cracked throatily as she went for the biggest lie of all. 'I *do* want that divorce.'

In the silence that followed the absurd tragedy of the situation caught her in its grip. Here she was desperately trying to persuade him into a course of action that would break her heart. To be separated from him at her own insistence when he had even seemed prepared to prolong the marriage was the epitome of irony. But she had seen the anger in his eyes, had felt the grip of steel on her shoulders as he willed her to deny his paternity, and had watched his shoulders sag with relief as she told the abortion lie. She didn't want a marriage based on guilt and mistrust, anger and reluctant duty. She would want Darcy coming to her willingly, without compulsion. . .happily, with love, and that could not be. He had no love to spare. She had seen that in his eyes at Heathrow Airport.

'You see,' she said with the calm of hopeless acceptance, 'it's all over.'

He phoned for a mini-cab then, and helped her

bundle a mistrustful Ali into his basket. 'I shall miss the old blighter,' he muttered.

To Jem's suspicious eye he seemed to be dangerouly bland in his cool preparation for her departure, as if the moment she was through the door he was going to cut an unseemly caper through the hall, whooping and hallooing at his close escape. But she realised that, with her fragile hold over emotion, she was liable to imagine all kinds of unlikeliness going on behind the cold mask of his face. Wasn't she herself schooling her own features just as assiduously?

With stiff formality they faced each other at the door.

'So, my protegée is leaving the nest.' He eyed her bowed head speculatively. 'You always were an independent cuss, weren't you?'

There was a slight pause as she tried to think how she could cut short this agonising farewell, when he held something out to her. 'Try to come if you can. I think you'd be pleasantly surprised.'

Jem didn't know how she brought herself to look into his eyes, but something, some surge of power, compelled her gaze upward. Behind the wry gleam in his periwinkle eyes there flickered a glimpse of yawning desolation. . .so brief as to be phantasmal, so deep and aching as to be the stuff of nightmares.

Almost unknowingly she held out her hand and grasped the envelope he offered her, and without a word turned and walked down the garden path.

Round the corner she came to sufficiently to attempt to haggle with the cab driver.

'Drop me off at the tube, please. I'm afraid I haven't got enough money for the fare to Streatham.'

'Oh, the gen'leman's payin', darlin'. Said to put it on

'is account. Lie back and enjoy it, that's what I allus says!'

So, however unwillingly, she allowed Darcy to pay for her eviction from his life.

London in spring had a charm all its own, but it was wasted on Jem that day. She couldn't believe the foolish thing she had done. As the dappled light flickered through the trees she stared blindly at the streets whizzing past and cursed herself for a fool. Why hadn't she grasped that tiny tendril of hope that he'd offered her? What had made her so proud an idiot as to refuse the one thing she would die for? To be near him. . .Live with him and bear his baby. Have the two of them, father and child, and. . .

The fantasy faded. . .And know that his love was forever denied her, she thought sadly. She shifted uncomfortably in the seat, telling herself to snap out of this useless conjecture. He was lost to her. She wanted him, but someone else had prior claim, and agonising over it would only prolong the suffering. As she brought her hands up to her face to try to wipe away the vision of him, the envelope he'd thrust at her fell with a plop to the floor.

Curiosity wormed through her apathy, and slowly she bent to pick it up. A flash of anger seared her as she suddenly realised what it most probably contained, and she was just about to tear the thing in half, unopened, mortified that he could think she would take money from him, when the feel of it made her change her mind.

'Darcy Lister invites you to a private view of an exhibition of his latest work,' read the ostentatious card, and below, in his inimitable, flamboyant script, 'I have a surprise for you. . .D'.

A surprise? What could it be?

But even as her heart tripped with irresponsible hope she knew that it was doomed. Any exhibition of Darcy's work would be organised and attended by the light of his life, Venetia Pitt. She would be there, stroking his ego and pushing his sales, while at the same time staging a spectacular burglary with Jem as prime suspect. A twisted smile spread across Jem's face at the thought, and she was vaguely proud of herself for still managing to retain a meagre sense of humour among all her pain.

No. She couldn't go. She no longer had the strength to fight the Scarlet Woman.

But that was the unkindest cut—not even to be able to see Darcy's work whose blood, sweat and tears she'd been so much a part of.

That night, even with Ali in his old familiar position by her pillow, she cried herself to sleep like a little girl with ear-ache—only now she was a big girl, and the ache had shifted to just left of centre in the region of her chest.

It was difficult enough to live through the week and a half leading up to the private view, but as the day itself dawned Jem found herself behaving like an actor going on stage for the first time to discover he'd learned an entirely different play from the rest of the cast. She was totally at sea. Nothing she said made sense. Her voice was two cogs behind her brain, and people stared uncomprehendingly at her as she spoke to them in what sounded like halting Latvian.

Nothing went right. Ali knocked her spectacles—her lifeline—off the mantelpiece and broke them. Her jeans zip refused, at last, to fasten, and the kindly lady at her first antenatal exercise class made the mistake of asking for 'baby's father's telephone number' after she had burst into tears for apparently no reason half-way through 'rapid pants'.

Suddenly it had been too much for her. The enormity of the task she'd set herself loomed like a megalith around which there was no path. It was easy to flash bravado about, but when the truth bit home, like here in the antenatal clinic, that she really *was* pregnant and that, unlike her, all these women in varying stages of glowing lumpishness had pleasant, safe, normal family lives to return to, it was as if she'd suddenly discovered, two seconds out of the bomb bay, that her parachute was torn. In four and a half months' time this tiny life was going to emerge into the rude world, and there would be nobody between it and starvation but herself. She was alone and, worse, desperately lonely.

She bought a paper on the way home. Sometimes it helped to read about people who were worse off than yourself. Sometimes it didn't!

She was idling through it, waiting for the kettle to boil, trying in vain to focus the larger print, when a photograph in the gossip column caught her eye. Surely she'd know that blonde hair anywhere? Grinning like the Cheshire Cat and flashing the loud diamond towards the camera was The Pitts, looking extremely smug.

Jem felt her heart quicken and tense perspiration break out on her forehead. She screwed up her eyes and looked closer. There was a man standing beside Venetia. A man with his back to the camera, kissing her. A man whose hair in the black and white photo looked almost as blond as Venetia's. Only it wasn't blond. It was white.

Underneath the photo there was a caption in large letters. . .'MARRIAGE FOR LISTER'S AGENT'.

With an inarticulate cry Jem let the paper fall from her hands. It had happened. They were married. She felt a burning nausea in her throat, followed by a ghastly desire to laugh. Venetia had won. Venetia was now Mrs Lister.

But something wasn't right. It took Jem some seconds to sort through the tangle of her distress before she realised what it was that didn't tally. There still hadn't been a divorce! Surely she'd have to have had some word, some decree, before Darcy could marry Venetia? Her ignorance on such matters was alarming. She supposed her solicitor had told her what would happen next, and how long it would all take, but she'd been too distraught to pay any attention.

An awful thought struck her. Suppose she'd received a letter and had left it unopened? For several days now she'd not bothered to open her mail. It all seemed to be unsolicited brochures for goods she neither wanted nor could afford, and that morning she'd been unable to see to read it anyway. Being without her glasses, she was blind.

With pounding heart she shuffled through the daunting pile, peering helplessly as fuzzy words danced foolishly before her. Eventually, after much fumbling and frustration, she unearthed something ominously official. The heading was just big enough for her to make out if she concentrated hard. Morris, Jenkins and Co. Her solicitors. This was it. The death knell to her marriage.

Try as she might, she couldn't read a single word of the letter itself, but she knew, deep in her heart, precisely what it would say. Dry and clipped, it would state unequivocally her new status as divorcee. She couldn't read the date, but it was obvious that Darcy had wasted no time in swapping wives. He must have been down to the Register Office the instant the divorce papers hit his hall floor.

She supposed she should be grateful she was no longer married to so callous an opportunist, but gratitude wasn't figuring high on her list of emotions. Her chief desire was to crawl under the duvet and, in the stuffy darkness, give vent to the tears of abject desperation that were welling up inside her. She felt as if there was nothing left to her. No hope. No future.

The doorbell pierced her wretchedness. Its clear tone cut through the fog of her abstraction, forcing her whirling brain to begin functioning again.

She couldn't face anyone. Not just yet. The thought of polite chit-chat brought a sob of derision to her throat, but the bell rang again. It had the insistent sound of determination, and Jem realised it was probably Elise from downstairs to check on how she was. Elise had appointed herself antenatal watchdog, and dropped in most days to make sure she was drinking enough milk and swallowing her iron pills. She'd probably call the fire brigade if she didn't get an answer soon.

Jem gave a bitter laugh as she folded the unread letter away from prying eyes into her bag. She suspected there was an ulterior motive behind the kindness. Common or garden nosiness. She was sure her neighbour would dearly love to know the identity of the father of her bump, but that was a secret that was never going to be revealed.

As she slowly descended the twisty stairs she resolutely tried to eradicate the bitter blow of divorce right out of her mind, sticking a bright, false smile to her face like a battle-flag. She opened the door with exaggerated flamboyance and stared straight into the clear blue eyes of Darcy Lister.

CHAPTER ELEVEN

'Hello,' said his deep, rich voice.

The sight of him stunned her. How could he possibly be standing here, at her front door. . .on his honeymoon?

'You don't know where I live,' she croaked uselessly, wishing it were true.

'No, I don't. . .but your erstwhile taxi-driver does. Wave to him nicely!'

Jem spared a brief glance for the traitor, but then had her attention grabbed again instantly by restless movement beside her.

'Right. We haven't got long.' He eyed her critically. 'You'll have to change. I won't have you, of all people, appearing in jeans.'

'Me? What are you talking about?' With surprise she noticed a new formality about him. A smarter, more polished air, but despite an immaculately cut grey suit, and the silver-grey satin of his shirt reflecting the glint of his hair, he still refused to bow to the convention of a tie. His neck and the slight V of his golden chest were still tantalisingly visible.

He ignored her expostulations. 'What will fit you now? Will this?' And as he bundled her up the stairs he tossed over her arm the loose ivory and gold crêpe de Chine dress he'd bought her in Hereford at Christmas. 'Go and have a quick bath and try it on. If it doesn't fit we'll have to improvise.'

He'd managed to propel her to the top of the stairs

before her protests had become strong enough to notice.

'What are you doing here? You're supposed to be on your honeymoon.' She found great difficulty in forming the word, but he seemed unaware of her constraint.

'Don't rush me, girl. Let's get this exhibition over with first. An artist must be there to greet his fellows and the critics. . .and, besides, we mustn't disappoint Venetia!'

At the mention of that name the blood drained from Jem's face and she had a moment's fear of passing out. But Darcy's strong arm under her elbow and the sudden concern on his face as he muttered, 'Are you OK?' filled her with a strange defiance.

'Of course I'm OK. Why shouldn't I be?' She moved away from him restlessly, frightened by her predictable reaction to his touch. 'Look, I'm busy. Tell me quickly why you're here, and then you can go.'

'To take you to the private view.' He spoke with calm certainty, filling her with unease. She knew how impossible it was to refuse him anything when he was in this steamroller mood.

'But I can't go.'

'Why ever not?'

'Well, because. . .I. . .' She groped clumsily for an excuse, caught on the hop as was usual when she tried to deceive him. 'Look, why do you want me there?' she blurted eventually, clinging to the maxim of attack being the best form of defence.

'I can't tell you just yet, Jemima. But I think. . .I hope it's going to be a rather special surprise. Do you trust me?'

She couldn't believe what he was saying.

'*Trust* you? *Trust* you? After what you've done to me? I was a fool to give you even ten seconds of my time. You have a tongue like silk and a heart like biltong. I could never trust you. Not as long as I live.'

He recoiled as if she had hit him.

'Yes, and you can look wounded if you like, but it won't change my mind.'

His eyes kindled. 'Will this change it, then?' he muttered savagely and wrenched her towards him, crushing her fragile resistance into a brutal kiss. Her long-atrophied senses leapt into iridescent life. A surge of half-remembered responses awoke within her to pulse through her veins, fighting all efforts to suppress them. With all her strength of will she tried to resist. She struggled against the pressure of his vicelike arms, managed a half-twist that was thwarted the moment his hand moved inexorably down to the small of her back and pressed her ever closer into the hollow of his body.

The solid roundness of her belly pushed uncompromisingly into his abdomen, but she tried in vain to disguise it. Her lips were burning under the bruising pressure of his, and she was fighting for breath. She raised her free hand, intending to try to prise herself away from his grasp but, to her horror, she realised too late that she was winding it helplessly round the back of his neck and up through the silver silk of his hair. Anger and confusion warred with the heady feel of sensual liberation. Her reason cried out to be released, but her body clung to him and her lips at last parted in surrender to the moist thrust of his insistent tongue. A moan of anguish escaped her. She knew she was mad to be allowing this. He was married. He loved someone else. He was just using her lack of will-power to manipulate her. The pain of his inevitable rebuff would be twice as hard to bear now that she had retasted the quintessential reason for loving him so blindly.

With painful reluctance they eventually pulled away from each other. Jem searched, shamefacedly, expecting to see signs of triumphant derision in the eyes that she knew so well could shrivel her with a mere glance, but what she did see there disturbed her far more. She had never seen Darcy look vulnerable before, but in the split second that their kiss hung in the air like an exclamation mark between them his eyes held the expression of a wounded animal, uncertain, exposed.

Involuntarily her hand reached out and touched his face.

'You are so good, Jemima Puddleduck. Such a sweet girl.' His voice was hoarse and the hand that covered hers all too briefly shook slightly. 'Jem, I'm asking you. . .nay, begging you. . .please come to the private view. I promise you, there's nothing there to hurt or upset you.'

Knowing she would never be any proof against him, Jem tried her last ditch stand. 'But what about Venetia?' she asked in a choking whisper. 'She won't want me there.'

The understatement of that remark struck her so forcibly, she felt constrained to grin shamefacedly, but Darcy looked at her earnestly.

'The blushing bride has other fish to fry,' he said, and Jem could have sworn, if she hadn't been so taken aback by the epithet, that she could detect a glint of derision in his eye. 'She won't be there, I promise.'

She stared at him in silence for a second, and then turned towards the bedroom to get ready. There was no point in fighting it. She loved him and would do anything to be near him, even if it caused her untold pain.

She bathed quickly, as he had demanded. She dressed in the sumptuous gown that he had provided. She alternately loved him and hated him with every breath, and dreaded the end of the evening when they would again part, she to come back to her spinster garret, he to fall into the bed of his 'blushing bride'.

They barely spoke in the taxi, except when Darcy murmured from deep in his corner, 'You're looking exceptionally beautiful this evening,' and she tried to brush it aside with a casual laugh. But casual laughs didn't come easily when you were rigid with nerves and there was a baby inside your stomach who suddenly decided that tonight was the night it was going to kick off for Tottenham Hotspur.

'Oh!' she gasped, pressing her hand over the disturbance. 'Good lord. . .it kicked!'

In one liquid movement he'd uncurled his great length from the corner and was beside her, pushing her hand peremptorily aside. As if to order, there was another faint eruption.

'Isn't that amazing?' he whispered in awed tones. 'It's a minor miracle.' He chuckled with suppressed wonderment, and as the taxi drew up outside a swish Bond Street art gallery their eyes met and he smiled a secret conspiracy. 'You didn't have the abortion.' He wasn't asking.

She looked away, knowing he'd known all along. 'No. I lied to you.'

'Yes, I know. Whatever for?'

'Isn't that obvious?' The pain in her voice fluttered round the cab like a caged bird.

He was about to reply when the door was flung open

and a short, balding man of late middle years and
extravagant habits extended his arm and endeavoured
to drag Darcy out on to the pavement.

'Darcy, dear boy. You've arrived. I thought you'd
never get here. Come and meet all the wonderful
people!'

'Right, Josh. . .in a moment. Let me introduce you
to the young lady first. Jem, this is Joshua Creasey. I'm
told he's sacrificing his reputation and his best wines
on my exhibition. It's his gallery, but no doubt you've
heard of him?'

Jem went a little weaker at the knees on hearing the
name of so famous a gallery owner, but as she timidly
offered her hand she found herself clasped to his bosom
like a long-lost friend and heard him boom into her
ear. 'So *this* is Jemima? Welcome, my dear. May my
doors be open to you forever.' And with a flourish he
led the way inside.

The first room was long and narrow, filled to bursting
with the type of people who dangled their wine-glasses
by the bowl and watched surreptitiously for more
influential companions with whom to be seen. As Josh
Creasey pushed his rotundity through the throng with
affable steel Jem caught sight of a couple of Darcy's
pictures through gaps in the crowd, and by the time
they had reached the main gallery she was thoroughly
confused. Surely they must be the paintings he had
been working on when she first went to live with
him. . .of the pneumatic students? But, from the brief
glimpse she'd managed to catch, hampered as she was
by near blindness, they seemed remarkably chaste
works. One girl even had her coat on!

There was no time for further speculation. A cry had
gone up the instant Darcy had stepped laconically into

the huge room that housed the main part of the exhibition, and Jem found herself pressed backwards into his protective grasp.

Flashbulbs popped along with a star-burst of champagne corks. Jem had a momentary panic about the repercussions of being photographed with Darcy and what the gossip columnists would manage to read into it. Venetia would start sharpening the knives. But as Darcy's friends and acquaintances began surging forward, adulatory words spilling from their lips, their seagull cries dulled her fears.

'Fantastic, darling!'

'Best ever!'

'The tonal quality of the nudes is almost sultry, you old devil!'

'I'd love to buy one, darling, but it has to go with the carpet. . .could you just tone down the greens a bit?'

Jem listened to the frenetic jabber like percussion above her head, wishing she could escape from this alien crush, but his hands on her shoulders held her tight.

'And who's the girl, Darcy? Where on earth did you find talent like that?'

'I have a vested interest!' came the equivocal reply. 'Jem, are you ready?' and as she nodded in confusion he led her through the knot of acolytes and into the centre of the room.

The walls were lined with Darcy's paintings, and as he was waylaid by yet another long-lost friend she had ample chance to study them. Startlingly bold, with vivid, intense colour, they displayed a draughtsmanship that was pure, clean, never lapsing into the banal. How she wished she had her glasses and could see them properly. The impression she got from so far distant

was of two distinct styles—before and after Tortola.
Even blinded by love and broken spectacles as she was,
she could detect flaws. . .particularly in the works
along the corridor wall, his earlier work. They seemed
stiff, lifeless somehow. As if the painter had been
working almost by numbers. She recognised some of
the girls—sitting demurely on the old chaise-longue in
his studio, looking to Jem's eye either defiant or oddly
bored.

And all fully clothed. Not a provocative nude in
sight. She sighed, realising how much jealous speculation she had wasted on these girls. He'd not been
terribly interested in them except as figures to paint.
She could tell that by the near perfunctoriness of the
brush strokes. There was one other clue as well. Not
one of them was painted more than once. She turned,
looking for any duplications, and came face to face
with herself.

Two whole walls were dedicated exclusively to paintings of her. She felt a profound shock at the sight,
almost as if the multiplicity of amber eyes were able to
read her soul.

She found she could actually chart the blossoming of
their ambiguous relationship just by following the
development in the paintings as they advanced around
the walls. She was amazed how well he'd captured her
moods. The gaucherie of that first, awkward sitting
giving way gradually to the mutual respect with which
they had once, so briefly, regarded one another. . .and
then finally to the payoff, to the explosion of visual
emotions that appeared to crackle across the surface of
his Virgin Islands canvases.

She was completely taken aback by the feeling of
raw power that emanated from them, and she even

forgot to be bashful at the sight of her own naked body
displayed so flagrantly for the fashionable of London
to ogle. It wasn't the subject that caught the attention,
she realisjed, it was the brilliance of the execution.

'I can see why everyone's glued to the Tortolan
works, Darcy. They're wonderful,' she murmured
humbly. 'Quite stunning.'

'Coming from you, that is a compliment indeed.' His
eyes were serious and the habitual banter was missing
from his voice. 'Come and meet someone who thinks
the same about you. Myles Cartwright, Fleet Street's
newest art critic. I think he'd like to use you as his first
scoop.' And he left her in the dubious verbal embrace
of a man who asked a lot of deep and meaningless
questions about her aims and ambitions and then
walked away, apparently satisfied with her hesitant
answers, leaving her utterly mystified.

'Darcy,' she muttered, turning to him, 'I think it's
about time you told me what's going on.'

'OK. Suspense over. . ."Come into the garden,
Maud."'

He grasped her by the arm and led her to a large
french window that took up most of the end wall. The
small garden beyond had been illuminated. Dotted
conspicuously about the terracing, picked out by spot-
lights, were. . .'My sculptures! Oh, Darcy, you've had
them all cast. I never dreamed what a difference the
bronze would make. But. . .they're not in your exhibition, surely?'

'No, my love. They're in *your* exhibition. Your first
one-woman show.'

With growing wonderment she hesitantly made her
way to the nearest—a lithe, aggressive portrayal of a
cat in mid-leap. 'Ali!' she breathed, stroking the bronze

back, barely noticing in her astonishment the tiny red 'sold' sticker at the top of the plinth.

She wandered, like a sleep-walker, between the sculptures. 'I never expected to see them again,' she breathed, realising in her growing joy how she had missed them.

As she studied them, averting her eyes from Darcy's keen look, she was trying to prepare herself for the inevitable moment when she would encounter the piece closest to her heart. The sculpture she had felt compelled to do, never realising till so long afterwards what deep and consuming love had guided her hands.

The blush was creeping over her face even before she had reached it. There it was. She drew a sharp breath and turned away.

Every naked limb, so achingly formed, every feature just as she remembered it, even to the fine crow's-feet beside the piercing eyes.

The pain of finding her sculptures like this confused her. 'Why have you done this?' she murmured brokenly, looking up beseechingly into the eyes of the real, flesh and blood being. 'You should have left me alone. I have to make my own way in life now.'

'Jem.' His voice was low and husky, and just the sound of it sent tingles of might-have-been soaring up and down her spine. 'I did it for you.'

'For me?'

'Of course! I found all this magnificent stuff in the conservatory after you'd left. You don't think I could allow it to rot there, do you? That would be a crime against art.'

'You could have asked me to remove it. I'd have got round to having it all cast one day.'

'One day!' he exploded, spreading his arms as if

drawing them all towards him. 'What if they'd been smashed? What if this baby of yours had killed that burning ambition? That was too much of a risk to take. I decided that, your permission or not, these sculptures were going to be seen. And look. . .' he grabbed her hand, leading her through the maze of gleaming figures '. . .look at the red stickers. See how many have sold. You're made, Jem. You're a success!'

Dazedly she followed him. 'How. . .how much did you put them down at?' she asked, wondering vaguely if they'd pay for a new pram.

He dived a hand into his pocket for a catalogue and watched as her expression changed from mild interest to incredulity, and finally settled into blatant disbelief.

'No one's paid *that* much, surely. . .for *one* piece?'

'They'd have paid hundreds more if asked.' He suddenly got into gear. 'For your next exhibition we'll have to do it all properly. Get you featured in the arty magazines. Have you interviewed for influential papers, really make sure——'

'You're sounding like Venetia,' Jem interrupted coldly, knowing that his enthusiasm was running away with his sense, and determined to keep *her* feet planted firmly on the ground, 'and I'm sure she won't let there *be* another exhibition.'

'She'll have no say in the matter,' Darcy said decisively. 'Your career is my concern. That is. . .assuming you still want a career?'

'Of course I do.' The bleakness of life without her work to get her through the day yawned before her for a split second. 'It's just about the only thing in my life, but. . .' She wanted to squash any idea he seemed to be brewing about helping her, but he wasn't listening. Still holding her hand with a grasp of steel, he led her to the statue of himself. It, too, sported a garish vermilion pimple.

She gazed at it dumbly, the wrench of parting worse somehow now that she knew money would replace it.

'A city gallery from up north has bought this one,' Darcy was saying. '*I* nearly bought it, but it smacked too much of vanity—even though you did flatter me.' He led her further round. 'So I plumped for Ali instead.'

'You've bought Ali.'

'Yes.'

'I'd better give you a discount for having looked after the real thing so often.'

He laughed, that splendidly infectious, joyful sound she had so longed to hear. 'No discounts. I did it willingly. But I'd have been even more willing if I'd known where you were. It was only when you came back for him that I had a chance of finding out.'

'You weren't supposed to find out.' She knew she sounded sulky and ungrateful, but it was hard to be gracious to someone who had, all unknowingly, reopened mortal wounds best left to heal naturally.

'Not find out where my own wife lives? Oh, come now, Mrs Lister, don't——'

His cruel taunt cut her to the quick. 'I'm not your wife any more, and you know it!'

His eyebrows twitched quizzically for a second. 'Whatever gives you that impression? I thought we were stuck like glue.' He lifted her hand, still trapped in his, as proof.

She tried to escape from his clasp, but seemed powerless against the draw of his eyes. 'We're divorced,' she whispered, uncertain all of a sudden. 'Divorced. I got the decree this morning.'

'How could it be the decree, you extraordinary girl? We haven't set foot in a court yet—and anyway, it isn't nearly long enough. Whatever you got from that solicitor of yours, it wasn't a decree.' He held her hand more kindly, stroking her fingers abstractedly. 'What did it say?'

She realised the split second after the words left her mouth how ludicrous they sounded.

'I haven't read it yet. My glasses broke, and I can't see to read.' As a defiant gesture to stem the flow of his sudden laughter she rummaged in her bag and handed him the envelope. 'Here, *you* read it.'

Sobering slightly, he drew out the letter, so painful to Jem's heart, and read,

'Dear Mrs Lister,
Further to our telephone conversation of 6th May, Mr Lister has since been in touch. You gave me to understand that he would present no objection to the proceedings, but he has, however, made it clear that he wishes to contest your application. Therefore, until I receive further instructions from you, the matter is in abeyance.

'I regret the delay in informing you of this matter, but I lacked a contact address until yesterday.

Yours etc. . .

'There you are, you see.' Darcy seemed remarkably cool about the whole business. 'That's what happens when you don't tell people where you live.' He paused and ruffled her hair with his old, familiar gesture, 'So, it looks as if you'll be lumbered with me for a while longer, doesn't it?'

It took an age for this latest bombshell to sink in. She was not divorced. All the agony that she had gone through was for nought. Darcy didn't want to divorce her.

But her brain still couldn't encompass the idea. How could it be? Everything she had overheard, all the things he himself had said to her, all had pointed the accusing finger firmly at divorce. It was what the whole marriage had been based on.

Suddenly she realised that a stray tendril of thought had escaped the net of her careful control and was prodding painfully at a new notion. . .the hidden meaning behind Darcy's wish to contest the divorce. Could he. . .? Did he. . .? Would they ever. . .?

Desperately, to shut off crazy speculation, Jem held out her hand for the letter, daring herself to believe what he had just read, but terrified that he was tormenting her in some way. 'Wishes to contest your application.' That *couldn't* be right. Hadn't he said himself, after that disastrous night on Tortola, that it would definitely have to be divorce now? In her confusion she scanned the blur before her.

'It can't say that. . .' she muttered breathlessly. 'It can't. I saw the picture of you and Venetia in the paper. How could you marry her if you weren't already divorced from me?'

'Marry Venetia?' The words exploded from him, causing a couple intent on admiring Jem's sculpture of Baryeshnikov leaping through space to turn and stare. 'I'd never dream of doing such a suicidal thing. What-ever made you imagine I'd put my head into that noose?'

'You love her.' Her words were barely audible.

'I most sincerely do not. Who sold you that line of goods?'

Jem felt herself getting completely out of her depth.

She couldn't believe that for the past nine months she had been basing all her painful assumptions on the wrong premise. 'But she's just got married, hasn't she? I saw her.'

'Yes, she's married. But *not* to me! She and Max are now quarrelling happily over dinner at the Pompidou Centre, I shouldn't wonder—fantasising over the biggest avant-garde extravaganza ever launched, celebrated by their names in lights. A veritable pair of egocentrics. Perfectly matched.'

'Max?'

'Max! Maxwell Hardacre, whose gallery I always used to show at. It took me a long time to realise that Venetia had an ulterior motive in placing my work there every time!'

'You mean it wasn't you she wanted after all?'

'Oh, I wouldn't say that! I think she had her eye on any easy meal-ticket, and if I was personable with it, so much the better.' He grinned down at her. 'But Max is richer than I am, and more easily moulded. She abandoned any hopes of me just after Christmas.'

'Christmas? Why Christmas?' Jem was finding it difficult to assimilate all this startling news. The firm rock of her certainty had turned to sand. The barrier of Venetia's impenetrable presence had suddenly been removed in one swift stroke, leaving her floundering in helpless doubt.

'Because last Christmas I played a bit of a trick on Ms Pitt. Remember the hoo-ha about the Degas sculpture?'

Jem nodded, the memory of that strange incident flooding back.

'I came into the room to be faced with anarchy. Venetia being sweetly reasonable, you white-faced with righteous indignation, and poor old Ali in the dock. I knew he hadn't done it, so there was only one thing for me to do. I confessed to a crime I didn't commit.'

'What?' Jem cried. 'You didn't break the ballerina's finger?'

'No. . .Well. . .not there and then. I did break it years ago, when I was a very young boy, and I surreptitiously stuck it back on again with fish-glue. . .But not since that time, no!'

'You mean it was wonky anyway?'

'Yes. Probably just fell off in the breeze, or more likely Venetia bumped it by mistake and then realised how she might be able to make capital out of a sticky situation. She's never one to miss too many tricks like that, you know. She thought perhaps she could blot your copy-book with the family.'

'I knew it!' Jem breathed. 'But why didn't you tell me?'

'I thought, wrongly, that my confessing to the crime would cause things to blow over. I obviously miscalculated the hurt she'd caused you. I'm sorry about that. It struck me then that Ms Pitt and I were going to go our separate ways just as soon as our contract ran its course. It terminated last week, and with it my association with Venetia. So, you see, you've nothing to fear from the new Mrs Hardacre now.'

'But,' Jem still wasn't sure she could believe him, 'you slept with her even though you disapproved of her?'

'I've never slept with her in my life. What a ghastly thought! When was I supposed to have committed that act of gross masochism?'

'On Christmas Eve.' Her voice shook with uncertainty. 'You were away for ages. . .and then, you remember, you told me that you were going to sleep somewhere more comfortable on the day I left as well. I automatically assumed——'

He tapped her nose quizzically. 'It seems that this led you along the wrong path, Miss Pry. On Christmas Eve I was playing Father Christmas. Six sets of presents to wrap and distribute take a long time. . .and, if I remember rightly, I was going to take over Clarissa's room, because they left the same day that you disappeared. There, you see. Nothing more gruesome than that. Is my spotless reputation still intact?'

With a sigh of self-disgust Jem turned away. What a lurid picture she had conjured just from a few misconstrued remarks and a deep mistrust that had festered since her first disastrous introduction to Venetia. True, Venetia had been gunning for her, but now she looked back she couldn't honestly pinpoint one incident that told of any closeness between Darcy and Venetia. It had all been manufactured by her own jealousy.

Suddenly the enormity of her stupidity struck her. 'You'll have to forgive me, Darcy. I. . .I think I'd like to sit down,' she breathed, not daring to meet his eye.

His quizzing air vanished instantly. 'Jem, are you all right? Is it the baby?' And he placed his arm tenderly round her waist and led her to a seat in a secluded corner of the garden. 'Can I get you a drink?' and as she shook her head, 'Are you warm enough? Let me——'

'I'm fine, honestly, Darcy. I just needed to sit down. This evening has been. . .a bit. . .disturbing, that's all.'

He sat down beside her, gently wrapping his jacket round her shoulders. 'Yes, to suddenly find that you're not footloose and fancy-free as you imagined must be a sight unnerving, I suppose. And that you're famous to boot. But to tell you the truth, Mrs Lister, it was a bit of a shock to me to find you trying to cast me up on the rubbish heap of divorce in my absence without so much as a verbal warning. What was all that about?'

It had never occurred to her that he might be upset by her precipitate filing for divorce. After all, hadn't she overheard. . .but of course, what she had overheard had been completely innocuous, she knew that now. Thinking back, she realised that her highly strung emotional state had completely obscured rational thought when she had overheard him discussing Venetia's marriage over the phone. She ought to have had more respect for him, more trust.

Filled with penitence, she turned impulsively to him, taking his hand. 'Oh, Darcy, I'm so sorry. I didn't mean to hurt you, but you'd said we'd have to divorce, and I thought, you see, that. . .well. . .' She found herself tripping over the words, unable to tell him in case she revealed too much of the true motive behind her impulsive action.

'Shall I tell you what you thought, my Jemima Jane? Shall I tell you now how much I've figured out since finding myself alone in that cheerless house with only the dejected Nathan for company?'

She gasped, trying to remove her hand once again from his clasp, feeling a cool dread mingling with the warmth of his pleasurable touch. What secrets was he about to expose? She couldn't bear the thought of being impaled on a pin like a butterfly, the pathetic, secret love she had guarded so defiantly revealed for his intellectual pity. But the fascination of his voice overruled the tremor of her heart.

'I didn't realise that that idiotic phone call I had from Venetia would cause you so much distress. That's what

it was, wasn't it?' As she nodded dumbly he groaned.
'I thought so. What a fool I was not to realise.
So. . .you thought I would just come back home from
the States with an eviction order all neatly made out
for your removal, bag and baggage, forthwith. . .and
expect to go to your solicitor the next morning, so that
I could marry that formidable mouth Ms Pitt in a
matter of months? Is that it?'

Again she nodded, quite unable to utter. So far he
seemed to have overlooked the one thing that would
have made this of such imperative importance to her.
That she loved him. She prayed silently that it would
never occur to him.

'And then to find out in the middle of all that that
you're expecting my baby! You poor girl. You must
have felt so alone. What did you think I'd do?'

The timbre of his voice had been lulling her into a
false sense of security, but she recollected herself just
in time.

'*If* it had been your baby, and *if* I'd played the
injured innocent, I think I could have forced you into
staying married to me for the sake of the child. Your
sense of duty would have compelled you to, I'm sure.
But it's not, and I'm not. . .so you see. . .you don't
have to. I'm not asking you to give up your freedom
for someone else's baby.'

'I see, and this. . .what was he? A chap at a party,
you said? What was his name? What did he look like?
He must have really swept you off your feet, and yet
you never even thought to tell him he is going to be a
daddy? Don't you think *his* sense of duty might compel
him into some sort of gesture of help towards you?'

She hated the lie. With him sitting there beside her,
so close, the warmth from his body penetrating the soft

fabric of her dress, she could feel the interrogation of his eyes seeking to bore through her averted eyelids.

'I. . .I told you. . .I was drunk. . .I don't remember anything about him. We. . .I. . .He. . .' She raised her eyes for a split second and knew that she was doomed.

His voice was rough. His hands on her shoulders tightened painfully. 'He! He waited until you were at the lowest, most defenceless moment of your life, didn't he? Bereaved, lost, frightened by the storms raging in your head and in the elemental darkness outside. Then he took you in his arms, so trusting, so grateful, so softly pliable, so adorable, and he abused you. . .didn't I, Jem? It was me, wasn't it? There was no man at a party. You never got drunk. You've never been drunk in your life. You don't honestly think I'd believe a lunatic story like that, do you? *I* was the one who stole your purity.' His voice was ragged with emotion. 'That's *our* baby growing inside you. And that's one of the reasons I want to stay married to you. For our child.'

He knew. He'd known all along. She felt a great sense of release as he uttered the words 'our baby'. At last she need lie no more.

But with that release there came something else. Something disturbing and fundamental. A raw need that stirred up latent memories, until now so ruthlessly suppressed. Of his hands in the hot darkness, seering across her naked flesh. Of his lips, wet and mobile, moving restlessly over hers. Of the ache she had felt ever since to know those lips again.

How she had longed to kiss and caress him. To love him. But all he felt was guilt. That most destructive of emotions. How could she show him? What could she say to make him believe that she had wanted him as much as he had wanted her? That he was not to blame?

'I'm not very good at lying, am I? It *is* your baby. It's very bad luck, me getting pregnant like that from just one. . .just once, but. . .well. . .I did.' She looked down at her hands, unable to meet his piercing stare. 'I. . .I. . .enjoyed it, you know. Please don't feel guilty about it. I was as much to blame as—no, that's wrong, blame's the wrong word. I'm just as responsible as you, so please, let me have the divorce. I don't want you to be tied to me because of some misplaced feeling of obligation. I know I——'

'Jem!' She felt the cool of his hands circling her face. 'Look at me.'

Slowly, reluctantly, her eyelids fluttered upwards and she found herself locked into the power of his gaze. It was as if his eyes were mirrors reflecting the message that she knew her own must be sending.

'To be married to you is no obligation. I'm not a martyr bent on self-destruction when I say I don't want a divorce. I *want* to be married to you. I've *wanted* to be married to you from the first time I painted you. That night of the storm in Tortola was the most magical of my entire life. I've never felt such emotion, such elation. You were—are—perfection.'

She gave an incoherent little cry, her heart beating uncontrollaby as his words soared through her consciousness, but he silenced her, placing the palm of his hand gently across her mouth. She could hardly bear to go on listening to him in case, again, she was getting it all wrong. That the meaning was somehow at odds with the words.

'No, let me finish. It's taken me so long to work myself up to this, I've got to tell you it all now.

'When I saw the ghost of your skin through the blackness of that awful night something in me snapped. You were so vulnerable. I'd wanted you for months. I'd felt how you were growing under my skin, filling my thoughts, making it impossible for me to concentrate on anything but you. But it was your arms so trustingly round my neck that night, the smell of your hair. You'd been difficult enough to resist at Christmas. There, at Tamarind Hall, with the grotesqueness of the world outside emphasising just how perfect you were, well. . .'

He paused, running a trembling hand through his shining hair, never taking his eyes off her.

'I know I said afterwards that we'd have to divorce, but I must have been crazy. I suppose I was trying to punish myself for having seduced you like that when your defences were down. Well, I certainly succeeded. I've been living in dread of it ever since, and I can't bear the thought of losing you. It's quite simple, you see, Jem. I love you.'

He spoke quietly and vibrantly, and it took Jem a second to comprehend what he had said.

'Oh, no,' she whispered.

'I know, I know. I've gone and complicated the whole issue, haven't I? It was meant to be purely business, a marriage of convenience, but I'm afraid I've exceeded the terms of our contract. I fell in love. I've loved you for a long time now, and you don't know what it's been like to live through weeks, months of hopelessness, searching every day, desperate for a sign that you might return just some of the feelings I have for you. Knowing that you lived with me in disapproval, just waiting for the day you could escape.

'This confession has cost me a lot, Jem. I have my

pride, but I couldn't allow you to destroy the happiness of two lives, mine and our child's, by just walking out. I had to tell you.'

Jem was hardly aware that her hands had crept up and were covering his as they compulsively stroked her cheeks. She desperately tried to fight the waves of euphoria that rose in her throat, daring herself to believe the joyous things she was only faintly hearing through a buzz of confused elation.

'Tell me again, Darcy,' she murmured huskily. 'Please, my darling, tell me again. . .and again, and again. . .'

She saw the look of defiance in his eyes melt into astonishment, and then at last to a revelatory exultation.

'Jem?' he breathed, catching hold of her with sudden urgency.

'Shh!' she whispered, putting her finger over his lips. 'No questions. . .just say it.'

'Oh, I love you.'

His gravelly moan convinced her. With the tension of realisation mounting between them, her trembling voice broke through the last barriers of their imbroglio. 'You know, don't you? I couldn't hide it now if my very life depended on it. I love you, too, Darcy. I love you with all my heart.'

She felt his hands gripping her and heard the torment in his voice as he cried huskily, 'Oh, Jem, my darling! Can you possibly mean it?'

For answer she lifted her face till it was nearly level with his and parted her lips. 'Kiss me!' she demanded. 'Kiss me and find out.'

With a despairing groan he bent his head, crushing her mouth in his hungry desire to clasp her as close to his aching body as was physically possible. She felt all the inhibitions of doubt and requiteless love easing swiftly from them as his kiss deepened, delivering them at last into the shallows beyond the reefs of uncertainty.

'My darling,' he breathed at last, his lips still tantalisingly brushing the rosy bloom of hers. 'I never dreamed this could be possible. Never in my wildest hopes did I imagine you could feel the same as I did. You always seemed so aloof. . .so other-worldly. I read condemnation in your eyes with every move I made.'

'Oh, how could you?' The lining of his ill-treated jacket rustled as it slid from her shoulders. 'I imagined my eyes flashing semaphore love at you. It must have been the effort of hiding it from you that made me so disagreeable.'

He grinned ruefully. 'It's bloody hard work, isn't it?'

She giggled. 'What idiots we were. I never guessed for an instant. I thought you tolerated me, that's all. That perhaps you thought you'd boobed by marrying me because you'd found out, too late, that you. . .' She faltered in embarrassment. 'Well, you know. . .all that Venetia thing.'

Darcy shook his head and groaned. 'Yes. . .whatever possessed you? How you could read anything into that, I don't know. *She* was the one I barely tolerated.'

'I don't know, either,' she murmured in self-disbelief. 'But somehow, if you get the worm of an idea it just seems to burrow deeper, becoming more and more out of proportion the further it goes. I just couldn't get Venetia into perspective at all. She became my personal ogre.'

'Well, forget her, my darling. She's Max's ogre now.

I just hope the marriage lasts till the end of the honeymoon, that's all.'

Jem laughed, with a slight pang none the less that she cared not one jot about Venetia's happiness. How wonderful it felt to be free of her at last.

'Now there's a thought!' he said suddenly. 'We never had one, did we?'

'No, I'm sure we didn't. . .but what?' Jem caught the infectious lunacy in Darcy's sudden *non sequitur*, delighting in the happiness that shone in his eyes.

'A honeymoon! The seal on the knot. The gilt on the gingerbread. I never swept you off to Benidorm and a fortnight on the Costas, did I? How remiss! But let me make it up to you, my darling. Let me——'

'We had a *sort* of honeymoon in Tortola,' she murmured with a twinkle. 'Won't that do?'

'No!' he said with finality. 'On my honeymoon I want to sleep with my wife every night, thank you. Not just the odd snatch, once! Shall we go back there and try again?'

'To Tortola? When?'

'Now. Tomorrow. I loved it there. That's where I really fell in love with you.'

'We'd have to stay in a hotel,' she giggled breathlessly. 'Don't forget about the tenant at Tamarind Hall.'

He threw back his head and laughed. 'I don't quite know how to put this, my darling, but. . .*I'm* the tenant. I wanted to make sure you had enough money,' he hurried on as she opened her mouth to protest, 'and that was the only way I could think of without you finding out.'

'Well, of all the underhand, low——' she began, but

he silenced her by kissing his fingertip and placing it over her lips.

'Shh. . .You can tell me all that tomorrow. Tonight we plan our future together spent in an ancient house perched high above a subtropical ocean, where you can sculpt and I can paint and we can both love each other forever and bring up our baby far from the madding crowds of weary civilisation. How does that grab you for starters?'

'It sounds stunning. . .for starters,' she smiled, 'but I'm not so sure,' resting her hand on the bump that protruded so rudely between them, 'that our baby here will be over-enamoured of all the peace and tranquill-ity. He feels like a Welsh scrum-half going into a tackle at the moment!'

'Does he indeed?' Darcy growled, drawing her closer to him, kissing her so delicately along the line of her chin, around her ear, over the fluttering lids of her eyes that she melted to him, surrendering her last, minimal resistance in mindless pleasure. 'He'll have plenty of time for making his number after he's born. Right now it's our turn, and we've got an awful lot of catching up to do,' he murmured, biting the tip of her nose. 'I've wanted to do this for so long.'

But just as she was beginning to think that their secluded bench was perhaps not secluded enough for what he seemed to have in mind, he sat bolt upright.

'Hang on a minute,' he muttered accusingly. 'What makes you so sure that it's a boy? I want a girl. I've set my heart on a tiny, dark, cheeky pixie with the face of a bush-baby and the determination of a donkey, just like her adorable mother. You can arrange that, can't you?'

Through her laughter, Jem nodded. 'If you say so.

I'll do anything for you, my darling—anything in the world.' She paused then, for effect. 'Except perhaps giving up my sculpture. I think I might baulk at that.'

'I wouldn't let you anyway,' he said decisively. 'I've told you, after tonight I'm retiring to a Caribbean island where I shall let my wife earn the living. How about that?'

She grinned up into his mocking face. 'Well, Caribbean islands certainly seem to nurture your creativity. There are numerous examples on display tonight—some framed, others. . .' she patted her stomach '. . .incognito! But I get the impression that you're not going to be allowed to rest on your laurels, Mr Lister. In the not too distant future you're going to find yourself in demand for more of the same. What do you say to that?'

With his eyes burning the deep fire of a dormant volcano, he drew her to him. 'My pleasure, Mrs Lister,' he said.

H A R L E Q U I N
Romance®

Coming Next Month

#3073 BLUEBIRDS IN THE SPRING Jeanne Allan
After the death of her mother and stepfather, Tracy could have done without a
bodyguard—especially Neil Charles. Attractive but arrogant, he clearly held Tracy's
wealthy image in contempt. They sparred constantly but she fell in love with him just
the same.

#3074 TRUST ME, MY LOVE Sally Heywood
Though it went against her nature, Tamsin had every incentive to deceive Jake Newman
on her employer's behalf. Yet when it came to the crunch, she found that Jake's trust in
her was the only thing that mattered.

#3075 PLACE FOR THE HEART Catherine Leigh
Florida real-estate developer Felicity Walden knows the Dubois family's Wyoming ranch
would make a perfect vacation resort—but Beau Dubois refuses to sell. Still, she's
convinced that a cowboy's stubbornness is no match for an Easterner's determination.
Even though the cowboy is far too handsome for the Easterner's peace of mind....

#3076 RAINY DAY KISSES Debbie Macomber
Susannah Simmons knows what she wants—career success at any cost. Until she falls in
love with Nate Townsend. But her five-year plan doesn't leave room for romance,
especially with a man who seems to reject all the values Susannah prizes so highly.

#3077 PASSPORT TO HAPPINESS Jessica Steele
Jayme should have been devastated when she found her fiancé in another woman's arms.
But there was no time to brood over the past. She was too busy coping with presently
being stranded in Italy in the hands of attractive Nerone Mondadori....

#3078 JESTER'S GIRL Kate Walker
The moment he set foot in her restaurant, Daniel Tyson antagonized Jessica Terry.
Though she reacted to him as a stranger, there were two things she didn't know. One was
Daniel's unusual occupation; the other was that they'd met—and fought—once before.

**Available in September wherever paperback books are sold, or
through Harlequin Reader Service:**

In the U.S.
901 Fuhrmann Blvd.
P.O. Box 1397
Buffalo, N.Y. 14240-1397

In Canada
P.O. Box 603
Fort Erie, Ontario
L2A 5X3

HARLEQUIN
American Romance®

THE LOVES OF A CENTURY...

Join American Romance in a nostalgic look back at the Twentieth Century—at the lives and loves of American men and women from the turn-of-the-century to the dawn of the year 2000.

Journey through the decades from the dance halls of the 1900s to the discos of the seventies ... from Glenn Miller to the Beatles ... from Valentino to Newman ... from corset to miniskirt ... from beau to Significant Other.

Relive the moments ... recapture the memories.

Look now for the CENTURY OF AMERICAN ROMANCE series in Harlequin American Romance. In one of the four American Romance titles appearing each month, for the next twelve months, we'll take you back to a decade of the Twentieth Century, where you'll relive the years and rekindle the romance of days gone by.

Don't miss a day of the CENTURY OF AMERICAN ROMANCE.

A CENTURY OF
AMERICAN ROMANCE
1900's

The women...the men...the passions...
the memories....

Harlequin Supperromance®

THE LIVING WEST

Where men and women must be strong in both body and spirit; where the lessons of the past must be fully absorbed before the present can be understood; where the dramas of everyday lives are played out against a panoramic setting of sun, red earth, mountain and endless sky....

Harlequin Supperromance is proud to present this powerful new trilogy by Suzanne Ellison, a veteran Supperromance writer who has long possessed a passion for the West. Meet Joe Henderson, whose past haunts him—and his romance with Mandy Larkin; Tess Hamilton, who isn't sure she can make a life with modern-day pioneer Brady Trent, though she loves him desperately; and Clay Gann, who thinks the cultured Roberta Wheeler isn't quite woman enough to make it in the rugged West....

Please join us for HEART OF THE WEST (September 1990), SOUL OF THE WEST (October 1990) and SPIRIT OF THE WEST (November 1990) and see the West come alive!

SR-LW-420-1